R0084100809

Praise for Beth Vrabel's *Pack of Dorks* and *A Blind Guide to Stinkville*

"Debut author Vrabel takes three knotty, seemingly disparate problems—bullying, the plight of wolves, and coping with disability—and with tact and grace knits them into an engrossing whole of despair and redemption. . . . Useful tips for dealing with bullying are neatly incorporated into the tale but with a refreshing lack of didacticism. Lucy's perfectly feisty narration, emotionally resonant situations, and the importance of the topic all elevate this effort well above the pack."

—*Kirkus Reviews*, starred review

"Lucy's growth and smart, funny observations entertain and empower in Vrabel's debut, a story about the benefits of embracing one's true self and treating others with respect."

—*Publishers Weekly*

"Vrabel displays a canny understanding of middle-school vulnerability."

—*Booklist*

"Lucy's confident first-person narration keeps pages turning as she transitions from totally popular to complete dorkdom in the space of one quick kiss. . . . Humorous and honest."

—*VOYA*

"This book doesn't soft-peddle the strange cruelty that kids inflict on one another, nor does it underestimate the impact. At the same time, it does not wallow unnecessarily. . . . The challenging subject matter is handled in a gentle, age-appropriate way with humor and genuine affection."

—*School Library Journal*

"*Pack of Dorks* nails the pitfalls of popularity and celebrates the quirks in all of us! An empowering tale of true friendships, family ties, and social challenges, you won't want to stop reading about Lucy and her pack . . . a heartwarming story to which everyone can relate."

—Elizabeth Atkinson, author of *I, Emma Freke*

"A book about all kinds of differences, with all kinds of heart."

—Kristen Chandler, author of *Wolves, Boys, and Other Things That Might Kill Me* and *Girls Don't Fly*

"Beth Vrabel's humorous debut, *Pack of Dorks*, takes a fresh look at what it means to embrace what makes you and the ones you love different. . . . The novel is a must read for anyone trying to survive fourth grade or anyone who remembers what it was like. *Pack of Dorks* is the pack I want to join."

—Amanda Flower, author of
Agatha Award–nominee *Andi Unexpected*

"Beth Vrabel's stellar writing captivates readers from the start as she weaves a powerful story of friendship and hardship. Vrabel's debut novel speaks to those struggling for acceptance and inspires them to look within themselves for the strength and courage to battle real-life issues."

—Buffy Andrews, author of *The Lion Awakens* and *Freaky Frank*

"Beth Vrabel weaves an authentic, emotional journey that makes her a standout among debut authors."

—Kerry O'Malley Cerra, author of *Just a Drop of Water*

"Most commendable is Vrabel's focus on compromise and culture shock. Disorientation encompasses not only place and attitude but also the rarely explored ambivalence of being disabled on a spectrum. Alice's insistence that she's 'not that blind' rings true with both stubbornness and confusion as she avails herself of some tools while not needing others, in contrast to typically unambiguous portrayals. Readers who worry about fitting in— wherever that may be—will relate to Alice's journey toward compromise and independence."

—*Kirkus Reviews*

"Brimming with wit and heart, *A Blind Guide to Stinkville* examines the myriad ways we define difference between ourselves and others and asks us to reexamine how we see belonging."

—Tara Sullivan, award-winning author of *Golden Boy*

"*A Blind Guide to Stinkville* is a delightfully unexpected story with humor and heart. Vrabel tackles some tough issues, including albinism, depression, and loneliness, with a compassionate perspective and a charming voice."

—Amanda Flower, author of the
Agatha Award–nominated *Andi Boggs* series

CAMP DORK

Also by Beth Vrabel

Pack of Dorks

A Blind Guide to Stinkville

Pack of Dorks

CAMP DORK

BETH VRABEL

SKY PONY PRESS
NEW YORK

To my pack

Sky Pony Press books may be purchased in bulk at special discounts for sales promotion, corporate gifts, fund-raising, or educational purposes. Special editions can also be created to specifications. For details, contact the Special Sales Department, Sky Pony Press, 307 West 36th Street, 11th Floor, New York, NY 10018 or info@ skyhorsepublishing.com.

This is a work of fiction. Names, characters, places, and incidents are either the products of the author's imagination or used fictitiously.

Sky Pony® is a registered trademark of Skyhorse Publishing, Inc.®, a Delaware corporation.

Visit our website at www.skyponypress.com.

10 9 8 7 6 5 4 3 2 1

Library of Congress Cataloging-in-Publication Data is available on file.

Cover design by Brian Peterson
Cover photos credit Thinkstock

Print ISBN: 978-1-63450-181-1
Ebook ISBN: 978-1-63450-620-5

Printed in the United States of America

Chapter One

This was the biggest summer of my life.

Surrounded by my pack, we'd take on the world. Or, if Sheldon had anything to do with it, at least summer camp.

I looked through the pamphlet Sheldon had brought in for our last lunch period as fourth graders. On the front read CAMP PALEO. The campground was in southern Pennsylvania, hours from home.

"Why Camp Paleo?" I asked.

"Humpf." Tom, aka the world's biggest jerkface, made his usual snorty grunt as he walked past our table. Hard to believe he had once been my boyfriend—or worse, that I actually *kissed* his chicken-skin lips. "Camp Paleo? Shouldn't you guys sign up for Camp Loser?" he sniggered.

I jumped up out of my seat, making Tom stumble back a step. Sam grabbed my arm and pulled me back into my seat and started growling under his breath at the same time. Soon, April joined in. Amanda cracked her knuckles. Sheldon's growl came out more like a *yip*. Not really frightening, until you noticed the way the veins in his neck bulged. Tom's ears flamed red as he practically ran to the so-called cool table behind us.

"That just never stops being awesome." Amanda crossed her arms behind her head.

"Never," I agreed, smiling at my pack.

"So, back to camp." Sheldon shook in his dino-shoe-laced sneakers, waiting to hear what we thought. Sheldon has a thing for dinosaurs. And by *thing*, I mean brachio-saurus-sized obsession. (He even has me saying words like brachiosaurus. The things you do for friends.)

"I don't know." April chewed her lip. "It's kinda expensive. And what about my red belt?" She took a deep breath through her nose. April is the middle of five kids in her family and used to speaking in bursts. I could almost see a mental brake being pulled up in her brain as she forced herself to slow her words. "I can't miss a lot of karate or Miss Betsy won't let me test for the next level."

I shuddered. I couldn't blame April for not wanting to upset Miss Betsy, our purple-haired, walnut-shaped tae kwon do instructor. We both took classes with Miss Betsy, but the aging ninja clearly had greater expectations of April than me. Which was totally fine. April goes to class twice a week like me, but she's also in the invite-only sparring class.

"Camp's only for two weeks. And look, archery!" Sheldon flipped over the pamphlet and pointed to a picture of a girl holding a bow and arrow. April's bottom lip jutted out as she nodded. Archery is sort of ninja-like. Sheldon pointed to something farther down on the pamphlet. "And there's this blogging thing—" but Amanda interrupted him before he could continue.

"Sounds awful." Amanda tossed her pamphlet onto the table and took a huge bite of her ham and cheese sandwich. "Why does it say we have to bring a can of soup? I hate soup."

"You have anger issues. Everything sounds awful to you at first," Sam pointed out, but not in a mean way. Just the way you'd say ham is pink. Or Sheldon likes dinosaurs. It's just a fact. Everything makes Amanda angry. "I think the soup is probably for charity or something."

Amanda shrugged and picked up the pamphlet again, giving Sheldon the little boost of encouragement he needed.

"Live Like a Caveman! That's the second part of the title!" Sheldon bounced in his plastic chair. "Think about it, Amanda. It says we make our own dinners. I bet it's those giant turkey legs! And the camp is built on a site known for fossils. We could find real fossils!"

Amanda tilted her head, considering.

"And, um . . ." Sheldon's skinny leg drummed up and down, knocking the edge of his lunch tray. "There are meditation classes. They, um, are designed to help with anger issues."

"Cool," Amanda said. "I've been meaning to work on that." Sheldon let out his breath in a low *whoosh*.

I couldn't believe they were all going for this.

It's not that I didn't want to spend summer with the pack. In fact, I was counting on it. We'd swim in Autumn

Grove Town Pool. We'd go for bike rides and watch out-door movies. Maybe we'd build a fort or something. But this? My eyes snagged on horrible phrases in the pamphlet. HIKE MOUNT HARMAN! Hike? Up a *mountain*? Why? EXCAVATE FOSSILS RIGHT IN CAMP PALEO! I wasn't sure what excavate meant, but I was pretty sure it involved dirt. SWIM IN NEARBY LAKE MATILDA! Lakes are where fish live. And poop.

Plus . . . and this really isn't a big deal . . . I'm completely okay with it, but it could be an issue for the rest of the pack, because it's a *sleep-away* camp. As in, drop-you-off-and-see-you-in-two-weeks camp. And maybe some of us haven't even had, I don't know, a single sleepover. Ever. I mean, I haven't had a sleepover yet, but I'm not scared or anything. Especially not scared about sleeping in the woods without Mom or Dad. It wouldn't be a big deal at all. But my parents probably wouldn't go for it. That's all.

I scooped up a spoonful of refried beans to fortify myself before crushing Sheldon's dream. "I don't think I can do it. No offense, Sheldon, but there's a reason people *stopped* living like cavemen. Like, I don't know, toilets. Running water. And Google."

But Sheldon wasn't going down without a fight. He held up a long, pointy finger. "Camp Paleo is sponsored by TechSquare!"

"Are we supposed to know what TechSquare is?" It's always refreshing when Sam asks the obvious questions, sparing me the responsibility.

Sheldon rolled his eyes, the veins in his neck dangerously close to bulging again. "It's only one of the largest Internet companies in the world!" Sure enough, right after CAMP PALEO IS SPONSORED BY TECHSQUARE, the pamphlet read, TECHSQUARE IS ONE OF THE LARGEST INTERNET COMPANIES IN THE WORLD! CREATED BY COMPUTER TECHNOLOGY GENIUS ALAN BRIDGEWAY, CAMPS PALEO AND EMAGINE WERE DESIGNED FOR THE EMERGING GENERATION.

"We get an hour of screen time in the computer lab, guaranteed, every single day. Boom!" Sheldon whipped his hand in the air like a rock star.

"Don't ever do that again," I ordered.

"Huh," Sam said, like Sheldon's gangsta move convinced him. "I'm in."

What? You know how sometimes you turn your head so fast your neck sort of throws up inside and you feel hot juice running down the inside of your neck? Or maybe you're more careful about throwing your head around. But that's how fast my head turned. "You're in?"

Sam shrugged, a smile tugging the corners of his mouth. "It could be fun. Two weeks away from here, all of us together. You should do it, too." He leaned toward me, chocolate-brown eyes sparkling. "I *dare* you."

My mouth spread into a grin. It was a low blow, but effective. I can't resist a Sam dare. "I'm in."

Amanda put a fist in the middle of the table. "Me, too." Sam and I put our fists on top.

"Yes!" Sheldon added his.

All of us looked at April. She chewed her lip some more and glanced at Sheldon, who muttered, "Please, please, please!"

"I'll talk to my parents." She put her bony fist on top of the stack.

We threw our fists in the air and howled. Kids at other tables audibly groaned.

"Shut up, dorks!"

"Do they have to do that every lunch?"

"Ugh!"

Ms. Drake rolled her eyes but didn't say anything. Maybe she spared us the lecture because it was the last day of school, but I think the real reason is she knows it's her fault we have a pack. She had assigned Sam and me a research project about wolves, which led to our forming a pack of dorks.

My grin spread, if that's possible, when our eyes met. I could see our fierce teacher fight to keep the stern keep-it-down-or-else look on her face. Soon, though, she smiled back.

Chapter Two

I lugged an overloaded backpack up the street to my house at the end of the day. Ms. Drake made us take home every scrap of paper from our desks and lockers. I think my backpack weighed about the same as a kindergartener.

"Bye," April said without her usual gusto when we got to her intersection.

Each step toward my house was another step away from fourth grade. Why did this bother me so much? I mean, fourth grade was pretty much a black spot on my otherwise blemish-free life. I started the year being the envy of everyone. By the end, no one wanted to be me. Except me, of course.

This was the year I finally learned that being a friend is more important than having a lot of friends. (Funny, isn't it, that learning that brought me more friends—*real* friends, that is.)

Yet lugging my bag up the street made me feel more and more like all of the things that kept my pack of friends together was as thin as a wisp of cotton candy. I knew I'd see April during the summer, since we live only a few blocks apart. Plus, my grandma picks up April every Wednesday and Friday for our tae kwon do class. But what about Sheldon? Or Amanda? Our parents don't know each other well, and I never see them around town.

And Sam. He lived on the other side of town, was constantly busy being a superstar at gymnastics, and wasn't the let's-hang-out-and-share-our-feelings type of friend. He was more the dare-you-to-eat-that-so-called-turkey kind of guy. I couldn't imagine him calling me to chat. Would he ever want to just come over and hang out with me, Mom, Dad, and my baby sister, Molly? I made one of Tom's trademarked snorty sounds. Of course not.

So, when would I see Sam?

Camp Paleo might be my only chance. But I was pretty sure Mom and Dad would veto my going to camp as soon as I asked.

The only sleepovers I'd ever been allowed to attend were at Grandma's house, and even then Mom lectured Grandma about not smoking her long, thin cigarettes in the house, curbing the cussing in front of me, making sure I ate the occasional vegetable, and getting me to bed at a decent hour. (I never told on her, but Grandma thinks "sleeping" is "watching SpongeBob on the sofa bed.") No way would they be okay with me being away from them for two full weeks!

"You're seriously sending me to camp? You know it's hours away! And sleep-away, too, right?" I pressed my hands so hard against the kitchen table that the vinyl cloth stuck to my palms while Mom looked through the Camp Paleo pamphlet. Who were these people?

Here's the thing: I want to go camp. I do! Mostly. But I thought Mom and Dad would be a little more reluctant about shipping me off to Pennsylvania. And I sort of had the idea that if I couldn't go to the camp, the rest of the pack—or at least Sam—wouldn't go, either.

"It's for two whole weeks!" I exclaimed.

"Adios!" Grandma called from where she was eavesdropping in the living room.

"Mom! This is a *family* conversation." My mom sighed through her nose as she bounced Molly on her knee. "Sounds like a great opportunity. You might even find a fossil!"

My baby sister took a break from drooling all over herself to giggle at Mom's bouncing. Molly is only six months old and growing little teeth. They might be fangs. The tiny white spikes in her gums are dagger sharp, and growing them makes her act like someone who's turning into a werewolf. She twisted her shoulders and threw her wobbly head back to scream. Like a werebaby. I haven't shared my theory with Mom and Dad. Yet. But I should stick close by for the next couple of full moons.

"Gurghlup." Molly stopped screaming and shoved her fist into her mouth. She plopped back against Mom's chest. Molly can sort of sit up, but only for a few seconds before her head gets too heavy and she falls backward.

"It's super expensive, too," I pointed out. "And you've got all those early intervention sessions for Molly to pay for . . ."

Mom's knee stopped bouncing and her eyes narrowed. Even Molly stopped mid-gnaw and stared at me. "First of all, Molly's therapy is paid for through the state and our insurance. Secondly, you don't need to worry about finances. That's my responsibility, not yours."

"But shouldn't I be here at home? You know, to help out?"

Seeing Mom's fierce face, Dad grabbed Molly around the ribs and hoisted her up in the air, tickling out another giggle. A dribble of Molly drool fell from her mouth and onto Dad's cheek. I shuddered, but Dad just wiped at it with his shoulder. I think a few months of changing diapers and getting puked on has made him just accept disgusting things as part of life.

Mom pulled one of my hands from the tablecloth and squeezed it in her cool grasp. "We've got things under control. You don't have to worry about us."

I sucked on my bottom lip. I knew why Mom was being so serious. I finally leveled with her and Dad a few days earlier, sharing with them a lot I had kept hidden in the months after Molly's birth. Things about my former best friend, Becky, going secret agent, pretending to hate me so she could report back all the mean things everyone said about me. And that she soon stopped being my friend, even in secret, and presided over the Everyone Hates Lucy fan club. I also told them about how Sam was the only person who was nice to me for weeks, and how Tom and his jerkface sidekick, Henry, made Sam pay for that by humiliating him so much he threw up before school for days.

I hadn't told them at the time because I thought they had enough to deal with after Molly was born. She was born with something called Down syndrome. It means that it's going to take longer for her to learn things, and she might have other health issues, too. Like werewolfism. (I made that part up.)

Dad grabbed the pamphlet from the table, moving Molly to his hip. She rubbed her gums on his shoulder, soaking his T-shirt with more drool in seconds. "Says here that there's a scholarship application online. TechSquare sponsors a Paleo camper each summer."

"I saw that," Mom said. "But Lucy would have to blog every day about camp. I'm not sure I'm comfortable with that."

I rolled my eyes. Mom and Dad were such pains about screen time. I was only allowed to Google stuff if they were in the same room as me. I don't even have a smartphone!

"It *is* expensive," Dad muttered.

The sofa groaned as Grandma hoisted herself up and waddled into the kitchen. Grandma wears sandals year-round, even in the winter, since her feet are so thick, and her steps are gentle as an elephant's. *Plod, plod, plod* into the kitchen. Mom opened her mouth to repeat, "This is a family conversation," but Grandma held up a hand to quiet her.

"Ran into Helen Harris at the gas station," said Grandma, naming Sheldon's grandmother. "She was telling me all about this Camp Paleo. It shares the campground with some highfalutin camp for web geniuses."

"Camp eMagine," Dad broke in. "They spend the whole time making phone apps and programming. I don't think Lucy would be into that."

I nodded. "No way." I might be a dork, but I wasn't a geek.

"Of course Lucy couldn't hack it there," Grandma sniped.

"Hey!"

She rolled her eyes and pointed a finger loaded down with silver and blue-stoned rings in my direction. "Let me finish. Helen says that Camp Imagine—"

"*eMagine*," Dad muttered just soft enough to make Grandma sigh.

"—recruits old farts like me to help in the cafeteria. Lucy would go to Camp Paleo for free if I worked there."

"You'd do that?" Mom asked, her voice high-pitched. "Be a lunch lady to pay for Lucy's camp tuition?"

Grandma nodded, making her chins wobble. "Already applied. I'm doing it for me, much as anyone. What am I going to do all summer anyway? Lucy off at camp, Molly at that day care." Grandma was a little bitter that Mom and Dad put Molly in day care instead of having her stay with Grandma all day while they were at work.

"Maybe you'll meet a friend," Mom said, ignoring Grandma's day care jab. The comment struck me as odd. I mean, kids are always on the lookout for friends. But grandmas? Why would Grandma need a friend?

Grandma sighed and stood back up. "How do you think I'm going to look in a hair net?"

I popped up and ran around the kitchen table to give Grandma a squeeze. Getting through two weeks away from home would be a lot easier with Grandma working at the neighboring camp. She patted my back.

"You're welcome," she muttered. She waddled back toward the living room. "Those kids better love Hamburger Helper."

Poor eMagine campers.

Chapter Three

While I sat on the front porch waiting for Sam, Grandma inched by me, yanking on the handle of her overloaded suitcase.

"You—*puff*—could—*puff, puff*—help me, you know," she gasped.

I stood up slowly, already feeling sweat drip down my back even though it was barely eight o'clock in the morning. I pushed Grandma's suitcase while she pulled in the direction of her car's open trunk. Hers was the typical oldy moldy car, a long sedan with an oversized trunk, velvety bench seats, and speeds that could only reach 60 miles per hour. We'd probably get to Pennsylvania by my eighteenth birthday.

"When's your boyfriend getting here?" Grandma asked after finally wedging her suitcase in the trunk.

"He's not my boyfriend!" I sort of shouted.

"Then why are you blushing?" Grandma put her hand on her hip and stared me down with her beady eyes.

My cheeks flamed. "It's sunburn."

"Sudden-onset sunburn?" Grandma chuckled.

"There's his car!" I squealed, which only made Grandma cock a caterpillar-sized eyebrow at me. "My *friend* who happens to be a *boy* is here."

Sam's mom parked just behind Grandma, but for some reason, Sam didn't hop out like I thought he would. In fact, he and his mom seemed to be snarling back and forth about something. It was a little strange.

I felt my cheeks flare red again. Here I was, counting the minutes until I could see Sam, and yet he was just sitting there in the car, yapping at his mom. I hadn't seen him in a month! We had only talked on the phone twice, making plans to car pool to camp, and both conversations had added up to about seventeen minutes total! (Not that I counted on purpose. The phone tracks things like that, and I happened to notice.)

This was not going as I had imagined. Sam wasn't throwing open the door, rushing toward me, crushing me in a huge gymnasticy-strong hug. I stomped my foot, and of course, that was when Sam finally looked up.

He smiled through the windshield glass at me, but it wasn't a super happy let's-have-the-best-summer-ever smile. It was a sad sort of smile, one that I've seen way too often on his face in the past.

Slowly Sam eased open the back door of his mom's car. She didn't even turn off the engine. That was also strange. Shouldn't she at least have a good-bye hug for her son before he headed off to camp for two weeks?

Sam trudged toward me, head hanging low and hair hiding his eyes.

"Don't forget your suitcase!" I called to him, but Sam just kept moving toward me. "Dude. Your suitcase . . ."

"I don't need a suitcase," Sam said. "And don't call me dude."

"Duh. Of course you're going to need a suitcase. You are going to stink so bad after two weeks in the same clothes."

"No, Lucy." Sam shoved his hands into his pockets and met my eyes. "I don't need a suitcase, because I'm not going."

Thud, thud, thud hammered my heart. "What do you mean you're not going? Are you going to meet us there instead?"

Sam swallowed and rocked back on his heels. "Listen, Lucy, something came up. An opening at this incredible gymnastics camp in Stanford. It's a camp for regional champions. After camp, some of these guys go on to Nationals!" Sam's eyes darted back and forth across my face.

"How ... when ..." I couldn't seem to form more than one word of each question.

"It's invite only, Lucy." His voice sounded like Dad's when he pleaded with me to go to bed at night. "Someone got injured and the camp had this last-minute opening. I'm the one they called. It's—it's sort of a big deal."

Sam's mom stepped forward then. I hadn't even heard her get out of the car.

She gave me a small smile and said, "It's a huge deal. It'll mean propelling Sam to the next level of gymnastics, beyond regional. It's an honor that he was invited."

I nodded. "Congratulations." But it didn't come out sounding genuine.

"I'm sorry," Sam said. "I really am. I know I talked you into this summer camp and now I'm backing out. But if I don't do this . . ."

I closed my eyes, picturing the mantel at Sam's house—how it was crowded with trophies and pictures of him winning at competitions. I remembered the way he impressed everyone with backflips on the playground. And I also recalled how much Tom and Henry had used his talent to crush Sam's confidence ever since second grade.

"You've got to do it," I said. Sam's mom let out her breath in a long sigh. She smiled again and turned back to the car. "I mean it. Congratulations," I said again.

Sam did hug me then, a surprise squeeze that almost bruised my arms. "I didn't think you'd understand," he said, "but of course you do. Thank you!"

I wonder if tears can sometimes flow backward, down the inside of your face instead of burning your cheeks. Because that's what I felt like was happening, even as I forced my mouth to stretch into a small smile. "Have a great time."

Sam shoved his hand through his hair, flattening the curls. "It won't be fun," he said. "It's going to be nonstop work. But the best coaches in the nation will be there. Even some college coaches."

"Dude. We're going into fifth grade. College? Really?"

"Seriously. Don't call me dude." But Sam grinned. "Really. College coaches. Gymnastics is weird like that." He pulled a piece of paper from his back pocket. "Here's my email address. I'll check it every day, 'cause you're going to get an hour of screen time at Camp Paleo. You can keep me updated on the pack. We have Wi-Fi at camp, so we can Skype, too."

This time my smile was easier to fake. He still cared about the pack. "I'll email you, but I don't think I'm going to go to camp. I'll stay home." The only reason I even agreed to live like a caveman for two weeks was because Sam was going to do it, too. If he wasn't going, neither was I.

I yanked my little suitcase out of the trunk, hearing Grandma's heavy steps plod up behind me. Both she and Sam said, "No!" at the same time.

My head whipped between the two of them.

"Oh, you're going, missy." Grandma pulled the suitcase back out of my hand, threw it in the trunk like it was as light as a pillow, and slammed the door.

"You've got to go!" Sam yanked on my other hand. "You can't change your plans because of me."

I bristled. "It's not *just* because of you."

"Come on, Lucy. You've got to go. I dared you."

"You dared me to go *with* you. You're not going, so I'm not going."

Grandma crossed her arms, sending the half-dozen or so necklaces strung around her neck rattling. "No, no, no. None of that business. You're *not* going to be one of those love-struck girls who only does what her boyfriend does. Not *my* granddaughter."

"Grandma!" I hissed. "He's not my boyfriend."

Sam's face flushed and his head jerked back like he'd been slapped. "Yeah," he mumbled. "We're just friends. But you're going."

"Fine," I snapped.

"Fine." Sam nodded.

We stared at each other for a second.

"Say good-bye to your boyfriend, and let's hit the road," Grandma finally said.

My life was ruined.

Chapter Four

Do you know what Grandma listens to on long car rides? Public radio.

Do you know how long I can listen to public radio before zoning out? I'm not sure, either. It all happened so fast. One minute, Grandma was cackling along to this old man talking about fixing cars. The next, Grandma's ancient old car jerked to a stop.

"We're here, Toots," said Grandma, stretching her arms. I rubbed at my eyes, feeling like Molly as I wiped some drool off my cheek. I caught Grandma's glance, eyes wide, in the rearview mirror and looked around myself.

A wooden sign at the edge of the stone and dirt parking lot had WELCOME TO CAMP PALEO painted on it in green letters. A dirt trail led into the woods beside the sign.

A bunch of teenagers in matching olive-green T-shirts stood around the sign holding clipboards. I heard high-pitched giggling and looked around for Becky, my former best friend who pretty much tried to destroy my fourth-grade life. But Becky, thank goodness, wasn't here. The laugh was from one of the teenage camp counselors. This girl wore a bright pink headband, her lips were the same glossy pink, and she clapped her hands when Grandma and I stepped out of the car.

"Another camper wamper! If your last name begins with an *A* through *F,* you're with me!" *Clap, clap, clap.* That meant April, Amanda, and I would be in the same cabin, which should've thrilled me, but I just sort of shrugged.

Grandma elbowed me. "I know you're bummed about your boyfriend—I'm sorry, your *friend* who's a boy—but time to get over it." Grandma rolled my suitcase to the overly happy camp counselor. I stretched a little beside the car, looking around for my pack.

Just then, a huge brown van thundered down the path toward the parking lot. Right behind it was a sleek, white sports car, top pulled down, kicking up the dust.

I rubbed some of the dirt out of my sleepy eyes and trudged on heavy feet behind Grandma toward the counselor. She had written her name—Jessica—on a nametag plastered to her T-shirt. The "a" was an enormous smiley face.

The perky counselor's real face fell a smidge as she glanced at me. I could sort of see why. I had caught a glimpse of myself in Grandma's car window reflection. My sweaty bangs were splattered across my forehead. Dust from the passing cars caked my cheeks. And my suitcase was a hand-me-down from Mom's college days. The handle was duct-taped to the case. And then there was Grandma, in her tie-dyed muumuu, smelling like the cigarettes she must've snuck while I was sleeping. Grandma grabbed a wet wipe out of her purse. "Clean up your face a little, Toots," she whispered.

A few seconds later, both of us turned as the brown van shuddered to a stop. Once I accidentally-on-purpose stomped on a spider and a million little baby spiders poured out from underneath its body. In a much less creepy way, people seemed to pour out of the van. I knew right away it was April's family from the way her younger brother Scrappy screamed out of a window, "Hi, April's friend!" Her teenage sister rolled her eyes and leaned against the side of the van. I could see through the open door that her other brother was sleeping in the middle row. Mr. Chester and Mrs. Chester, with the baby on her hip, pulled bags from the back of the van. Scrambling over the back row to climb out of the trunk came April, Amanda, and Sheldon. They were all giggling.

"Guys!" I waved to them as Grandma checked over my registration with Jessica. But they were so busy having fun and divvying up their luggage, they didn't see me. I noticed April's hair was perfectly smooth and she wasn't the least bit sweaty or dirty. I smoothed my hair a little. I waved a little harder, standing on my tiptoes.

My pack still didn't see me, but the kid getting out of the sports car did. He slipped his sunglasses up to the top of his head and winked, clearly thinking I had been waving like crazy at him. For real. He waved back.

"No!" I started to say, but bit off the comment. I didn't want to start off camp being the jerk who waved at a kid and then said, "No, not you." I felt my face burn bright red. Not sure what to do, I just sort of hid behind Grandma.

But this kid strode forward, somehow kicking a hacky sack from knee to shoulder to ankle and back again as he walked. "Hey," he said with a nod. "I'm Jer."

Jer smiled, his teeth straight and white against his dark brown skin. I caught just a glimpse of his green eyes as he lowered sunglasses back over them. "What's your name?"

Grandma nudged me to answer and maybe, I don't know, stop standing against her. But before I could answer, my pack finally saw me.

"Lucy!" April shouted. "You're here!"

"Nice to meet you, Jer. I'm Lucy. Bye!" I said in a gush, then darted over to my friends.

Later, after we said good-bye to our parents (and me to Grandma) and lugged our bags down the path through the woods to our campsite, I felt a little bad that I had sort of brushed off Jer. I knew I had somehow given him the impression that I *liked* him, if you know what I mean. Probably the best thing to do would be to just not talk to him for a few days.

And besides, I had bigger things to worry about. Like living among spiders.

Camp Paleo cabins were seriously just open log A-frames, with spiderweb drapery. April took the bunk above me and Amanda the one to her right. Under Amanda was a skinny girl named Megan who hadn't spoken yet. She's Korean, like Sheldon. Maybe she doesn't speak English? On the other side of them was a bunk bed with Kira on the top bed. I don't actually know her yet, but I know I don't like her. She brought an enormous designer makeup bag to camp. Our counselor, Jessica, who slept under Kira, asked her how much something like that costs, and Kira replied, "Way more than you can afford." Seriously.

Kira's twin brother, Ash, seems okay, though. He's Sheldon's bunkmate in the boy's A-frame nearest ours, and I didn't hear him complain once when Sheldon went on and on (and on) about the types of fossils they might find at the archeological site.

After unpacking all of our stuff in our so-called cabins, we made our way to the computer lab, which was right outside Camp eMagine, for our screen time. It was too dark by then to see much of the techy camp, other than it featured actual buildings with electricity, judging from the light coming from windows. I hoped Grandma was okay.

Everything cool here. Getting settled, I emailed Sam.

But really, I already missed home.

One day down at Camp Paleo! So far, camping like a caveman means eating horrible food, living among spiders, and trying not to fart in your sleep. We're supposed to go on a hike today and then check out the archeological site. We might even trapeze pass the lush grounds of Camp eMagine. I hear they have such luxuries as running water and flushing toilets! Imagine!

We're off to the excavation site today. You can keep the fossils; I'm all about uncovering more about yours truly. What are you going to learn during these two weeks of cave—man living? What questions do you have, fellow campers and noncampers alike? Ask away!

Xoxo,
Your Super—Secret Camp Paleo Blogger (SSCPB)

"Well, whoever SSCPB is, she's a girl." Sheldon held his nose and swallowed a mouthful of watery orange juice stuff. A printed copy of the SSCPB's blog post was posted at our eating area so we didn't have to wait until that night's screen time to see what the mystery blogger had written. I took a sip of the juice. I'm not sure any actual oranges were squeezed in the making of it. I grimaced. It tasted like lake water with a faint orangey aftertaste.

"What makes you say SSCPB is a girl?" Amanda crossed her arms and glared at Sheldon.

He shrugged. "The ex-o-ex-o. Guys don't do that."

Amanda pushed out her bottom lip while she thought about whether that made her angry. Eventually she shrugged and scooped up some mushy greenish-yellow lumps that Mr. Bosserman, our elderly camp director, called "eggs." Around a full mouthful of "eggs," she shrugged again and said, *"Kumbaya."* We kicked off our days here at Camp Paleo with meditation, which Amanda took very seriously. The yoga instructor told her that any-time she'd ordinarily grouch about something, she should chant *kumbaya* instead. Already, she must've said it a thousand times and it was barely eight in the morning.

"Some guys do!" April broke in. She took a deep breath and smoothed her hands along her legs. "What I mean is, sometimes guys do sign off messages with hugs and kisses. I think my dad might to my mom. It's not enough evidence to conclude that the blogger is a girl."

Amanda, Sheldon, and I glanced at each other under our lashes. We still were getting used to April's new way of talking. I know that sounds strange. I mean, it's not like she was suddenly using sign language or speaking Japanese. She was just talking normal. Only, not normal for April.

Since we got to Camp Paleo two days ago, April has been different. When I asked her about it, she said she was "reinventing" herself. I figured it'd wear off soon, like when Dad was going to reinvent himself by getting up early each morning and exercising like a madman. (Seriously, he said it was called the Lunatic workout.) That lasted three whole days. He went back to sleeping in and grabbing a doughnut on the way to work. But so far, April was sticking to her reinvention. I wanted to talk to Sam about it, but he was still practicing last night when our hour of screen time ended. The gymnastics camp was in California, with a three-hour time difference. I crumbled up my napkin and threw it on my still-full plate.

"I don't like the way you talk now," Amanda snapped at April.

I shuddered, watching Amanda scoop up another forkful of "eggs." I never thought I'd yearn for Autumn

Grove Intermediate School's turkey-ham. Or even Dad's maraschino cherry–glazed salmon. A cracker. Anything. But Mr. Bosserman insisted that part of Camp Paleo was making our own grub. So each day began with dunking our stainless steel cups into a vat of what was called juice. Then each campsite had to alternate making the meals. Today was the group of boys across from us. The boys had poured the liquid egg mixture out of a gallon jug onto a grill. They pushed the pieces around with a spatula until it was solidly mushy and then dumped it onto our plates.

Last night, we had hamburgers thin as pancakes served on wilted lettuce and a few carrot sticks. I don't know what kept me up so late last night—the rumbling in my stomach or Amanda's snoring from the bunk next to me. Or the fact that spiders lived right over my head.

"Okay, camper wampers!" Jessica bounced up to our picnic table, clapping her hands and sending her ponytail bouncing. I hate Jessica. I know, I know. Hate is a mean word. Fine. I *strongly* dislike Jessica. A lot. "Who's ready for a super-fun day, living it up like a caveman?" She did this strange little jig when she said caveman, widening her arms like a gorilla and stomping from foot to foot.

You know how perky Jessica was when I arrived at camp? She's like that all the time. Most of the camp counselors spent last night looking bored and playing with their smartphones. Not Jessica. She bounced around the A-frame adding "homey" touches, like posters of kittens and a braided rug. Then she made us sit in a circle and sing songs about paving paradise to put up a shopping mall.

At least I'm not alone in not liking Jessica. I'm pretty sure Mr. Bosserman would like to pave her mouth shut. He now stood over us, his arms crossed, scowling at Jessica. Mr. Bosserman's arms were almost as hairy as his ears. Maybe he took personal offense to the gorilla act.

"Where's the toast?" I asked.

"Cavemen didn't eat bread," he grumped, not even looking at me.

"I don't think they ate pourable eggs, either. Or had this orangey-juice-stuff-that-is-definitely-not-actually-o-j."

Mr. Bosserman has a scary glare face. I swear, his gray eyes vibrated at me.

"Ha!" Jessica giggled. "Such a kidder, this one!"

Mr. Bosserman switched his scary eyes to her, not that she noticed. "Eat up," he snarled. "We're hiking to the archeological site today." His eyes widened at Sheldon's fervent, "Yesss!" and then he continued, "The hike's going to take a couple hours."

"Hours?" I glared up at the sky. Clouds trapped the hot, heavy air like a wet blanket pressing against us. It had to be a hundred degrees. Both of my cheeks were sweating and it wasn't even nine o'clock yet. "We're going to melt!"

"Fossils! Fossils! Fossils!" Sheldon cheered. I guess he was taking over for April's old way of talking in loud, one-word bursts.

"Come on! Quiet your brutzing." Mr. Bosserman clapped. "We've got to get there before it makes wet."

Our heads swiveled toward him. "Before what makes wet?" Sheldon whispered. His eyes fluttered down to Mr. Bosserman's pants.

"Silly Mr. Bosserman!" Jessica bounced. She went to pat the old man on his shoulder, but he sprang out of reach with surprising old-man speed. "He means before it rains! He's speaking Dutch again. Mr. Bosserman," she sing-songed, "if you want the children to understand, you can't use words like brutz. Say 'stop complaining.'"

Jessica's perky smile wilted under Mr. Bosserman's poisonous glare. Finally he turned toward us. "Put on some sunscreen," he said and slapped a mosquito on his arm. "And some bug spray."

"Fossils! Fossils! Fossils!"

"Cavemen didn't wear sunscreen or bug spray," I pointed out.

Mr. Bosserman ignored us all.

"Have you noticed how grumpy Mr. Bosserman is all the time?" April asked as we kicked off our hike down a stone and dirt path through the woods. At least it was shady.

I laughed. "Kind of hard not to."

April giggled, too. "Like your grandma!" She paused. "I mean—"

"Yeah, I know," I interrupted before she could start over in her reinvented way of talking, which, seriously, makes every conversation with her last three times as long. "Maybe we'll see Grandma on the hike! Jessica said we'll pass through Camp eMagine on the way to the dig."

I stepped a little faster, thinking of Grandma. She had promised to check on me soon, but I guess she's been busy being eMagine's lunch lady. My throat suddenly felt a little smaller, like I was trying to choke down a rock. I imagined her heavy hand on my shoulder. I know it had only been two days—less than that, really—but I missed her. Maybe having her close by but not there made it harder, because no one else seemed homesick. I shook my head, as much to push away thoughts of Mom and Dad and my werebaby sister along with the mosquito nibbling on my neck.

"She and Mr. Bosserman should get together. Can you imagine?" April giggled again.

"All new levels of grouchiness!" I laughed. "I'm having a hard time imagining her cooking for those poor eMagine

kids. Once she convinced me she made fried farts and onions for dinner."

April and I turned to the snorting sound behind us.
Megan, the skinny silent girl from our cabin, covered her
mouth with her hand. So she does speak English—or at
least understands it. Megan's face flushed, and she stared
off into the woods around us.

April caught my eye and smiled. Maybe she, like me,
was thinking of Sam, who had spent years barely saying a
word. Maybe Megan was only shy until she had a friend.
We slowed down a little so Megan would be more with us
than behind us.

"Maybe we should introduce them," I said. "Mr.
Bosserman and Grandma, I mean."

"Fried farts and onions would be an improvement
over what we had for breakfast," Megan whispered just
loud enough to hear. All three of us laughed at that.

Kira, who'd been walking behind us, bumped into my
shoulder accidentally-on-purpose. "Ew, dork germs!" She
rubbed at her arm, then flashed me a huge grin. Or, rath-

er, smiled at April. "Just kidding, of course." She straightened her bandana-style headband and kept walking.

"We happen to *like* being dorks!" I called to Kira's back.

"Sure you do," her voice floated back.

I went to roll my eyes at April when I noticed she had her bangs pulled back under a bandana headband like Kira's. Her face flushed.

"What's with the hair?" I asked.

"What?" she stammered. "I always wear it like this."

"Since when?"

She shrugged, then purposefully walked forward, shoulders pulled back like Kira's in the distance.

Maybe it wasn't just her way of talking that April was trying to reinvent.

I stepped a little faster, trying to keep up with April's long legs. Soon the path smoothed out. The rocks and dirt gave way to blacktopped walkway. The trees thinned.

Sheldon pushed ahead of us. "Fossils! Foss—oh, *man*! It's just the other camp." He jerked his thumb toward a carved wooden sign: WELCOME TO CAMP eMAGINE.

Amanda let out a low whistle. She started chanting *kumbaya* under her breath and flexing her fists to stay calm.

If I weren't convinced a thousand mosquitos would fly into my mouth, I'm sure my jaw would've dropped as I looked around. Camp eMagine? It was everything Camp Paleo wasn't.

We walked through double metal gates onto a brick paved road. Adorable log cabins lined the sides of the drive. Each had flowerboxes attached to its windows with blue and yellow pansies waving happily to our starved, Camp Paleo–deprived souls. The lawns around the little cabins were emerald green. Trees taller than any I'd ever seen flanked the background. At the center, we passed a huge log cabin—more of a mansion, really. As we reached the back of the building, I spotted an enormous, crystal-clear pool, complete with sparkling waterfall and Jacuzzi.

"*Kumbaya! Kumbaya!*" Amanda's meditation sounded more like a growl as she hissed through closed teeth. "They. Have. A. Pool."

Suddenly my T-shirt wasn't just sweaty—it was plastered to me with the weight of my body's tears. I didn't *want* to swim in cool, clean water. I *had* to. I didn't even realize that my arms were rising, hands outstretched like I already was splashing in that gorgeous oasis.

"Do you mind?" Kira asked, sidestepping away from my fingers. "Besides, it looks like the pool is being used for whale training at the moment." She tilted her chin toward the pool and laughed.

There, floating in the middle of that little slice of heaven, was Grandma.

Grandma's bathing suit was this two-piece combo of orange and blue tie-dyed top and skirt bottom. Grandma floated with her toes and nose sticking up from the surface of the water. Her damp hair flounced around in the water around her head, not in its usual wild, kinky curls. Huge, round sunglasses covered her eyes.

"Grandma?" I gasped.

Even with her ears underwater, she somehow heard me and righted herself. Her tan arms sliced through the water as she swam to the edge of the pool. I rushed forward.

"Hey, Toots," she said, like all of this—me, roasting like a marshmallow on a stick while she floated in a pool when she was supposed to be lunch-ladying—was somehow, in any universe, okay.

"Aren't you supposed to be making some tater tots?" I snapped.

"Aren't you supposed to be digging up fossils?" Grandma hoisted herself up the side of the pool and swung her legs around. "Lunch crowd doesn't start until noon. I've got the mornings to myself." She wrapped a towel around her body, tucking it in like a toga. Something about how she said "to myself" lingered in the air a little. She had used the same tone to complain about Molly going to day care.

"Where are the other lunch ladies?" I asked.

Grandma shrugged. "Turns out, they've been here every summer for the past half-decade. They don't need another old fart like me hanging around."

I moved in and gave Grandma a quick squeeze, and only partly to get some of her cool sogginess on me. I squeezed harder when Kira snickered behind me.

"How's it going, kid?" Grandma asked.

I shrugged. "Food's gross."

Grandma started to reply but was cut off by Mr. Bosserman. "Ah, come on! Get moving, get moving, onest."

"*Onest?*" Grandma repeated slowly. It was like "one" and "first" mushed together. "Are you Dutch? Or Amish?" Her eyes were wide, like she had seen—or heard—a ghost.

Mr. Bosserman crossed his hairy arms. "What's it to you? Grew up outside Lancaster County, Pennsylvania."

"I went to Penn State," Grandma said. "Ended up marrying a Pennsylvania Dutch boy." April widened her eyes at me, and I shrugged. This was the first I'd ever heard Grandma talk about my long-gone grandpa. He and Grandma divorced before Mom was born.

Mr. Bosserman narrowed his eyes and stared at Grandma like he was sizing her up. "Ever had shoo-fly pie?"

"Sweetest stuff in the world." Grandma scrunched her nose like that was a bad thing. "Made me want to kutz."

Mr. Bosserman's lips twitched. "How do you like your pot pie?"

"Slippery. Of course."

Now, miracle of miracles, Mr. Bosserman grinned, wrinkles popping up around his eyes like cracks in concrete.

Grandma put her hands on her hips. "Know what I think I miss the most? Chow chow."

"Is she talking about a dog? Is this even English?" Amanda whispered to me.

I shrugged.

Mr. Bosserman shifted on his feet. "I got some canned, I think, if it isn't all gone. Maybe I'll root it up for you."

"I'd like that." Grandma smiled. "If you'd share it with me."

Wait a sec—was Grandma flirting? With *Mr. Bosserman*?

Grandma tightened the hold on her towel and looked Mr. Bosserman up and down, from his wide-brimmed safari-style hat to the short-sleeved shirt and the way its buttons pulled around his waist, then down to his heavy black shoes. She looked at him the way Mom looks at the poster of Indiana Jones hanging in her closet. Yup. Definitely flirting.

"Well, we've got get moving. I'll see you soon . . ."

"*Ich bin die* Irene," Grandma introduced herself.

"Harold," Mr. Bosserman said. He turned and clapped his hands together. "Get a move on, campers. We've got a lot more hiking ahead of us." And then, he whistled.

"Grandma?" I hissed.

But she ignored me, lowering herself back in the pool and floating backward with a little smile breaking up her pruney face.

"Do I even want to know what chow chow is?"

I could still hear her laughing as we trudged back down the trail.

Chapter Five

Each evening, we went for an hour to the computer lab just outside the eMagine camp entrance. Usually this was awesome—a chance to sit in real air conditioning with electricity!—but since we had seen the gloriousness of eMagine's camp earlier that day on the way to the fossil dig, I think I wasn't alone in feeling a little bitter. Sure, electricity was nice. So was not feeling a river of sweat run down my back for the first time all day. But it didn't compare to that swimming pool!

We found spots in cubicles behind PCs, except for the lucky few who had brought laptops. They got to sit at a long table. April, who had gotten a laptop before camp, was sitting next to Kira. Kira's laptop was pink. Gross!

"So, what am I missing?" Sam's face blurred for a second on the screen as he leaned forward.

I tried to ignore my sweaty, poofy-haired, bug-bitten mess of a face in the bottom right corner of our Skype connection. The only consolation was that his face also looked flushed and sweaty. I guess hours of gymnastics does that to a person.

"Not much," I said. "We looked for fossils today."

"I bet Sheldon was in heaven." Sam smiled.

I shrugged. "He sort of freaked out. You know that huge vein in his neck? It had a heartbeat."

Sam's laugh always comes in bursts, like he's shocked to find something funny. "What happened?"

I closed my eyes for a second, remembering. The dig area was just a dirty patch of ground on the side of a small mountain. A ring of yellow tape marked off the excavation site. We broke up into partners and used little hand shovels and garden rakes to look for fossils, except for Sheldon, who had brought his own geological tools along.

Amanda and Sheldon paired right away. Somehow April ended up with Kira, and I was stuck with Megan. I tried to scoot closer to the rest of my pack, but Mr. Bosserman snapped at us not to *rutch* so much, which Jessica cheerfully interrupted, saying it meant "don't bounce around."

Mr. Bosserman crossed his arms. "Chances are you aren't going to find much. And if you do, it'll be damaged. So don't get your hopes up."

All of us sighed except for Sheldon, who nodded and hunched over his patch of dirt with such intensity I could see his shoulder blades popping out against his T-shirt (which also happened to have a dinosaur fossil on it). "Fossils. Fossils. Fossils," he muttered.

I smiled, thinking about the squeal Sheldon would make when he finally found one.

"Well," I told Sam, "Sheldon found the first fossil, this little piece of rock with part of a leaf stuck in it. Anyway, he held it up, and everyone rushed him like he was an ice cream truck or something. Then he went crazy, screaming at people not to 'disturb the excavation.' Amanda lunged in front of him and made this little barricade."

"Ice cream truck?" Sam cocked an eyebrow.

"Sorry. Part of Camp Paleo's mission is apparently starving people."

It had started drizzling before we left the site. By the time we'd reached the bottom of the mountain, it all-out poured. Tiny rivers of mud ran through my sneakers.

The amazing smell of sloppy joe wafted from the open windows of Camp eMagine's mess hall as we trudged by on soggy, squeaking sneakers. The tantalizing aroma filled our nostrils and rattled around in our empty, barbecue-meat-deprived bellies.

"Get back here!" I heard Grandma bark to an eMagine camper. "You forgot your cookie!"

Cookie? How do you *forget* your cookie?

"Can we just—" I started.

"No." Mr. Bosserman didn't pause in his heavy strides, even though each Camp Paleo camper slowed to a crawl at the siren song of cookie.

"But—"

"No."

"Come on, camper wampers!" sang Jessica, though even her perky smile wilted a bit in the rain. "We'll have a great lunch back at our camp! What are we having today, Mr. Bosserman?"

"Jerky."

"What?" Jessica asked, her smile twisting.

"Beef jerky," Mr. Bosserman said. "And some apples."

"I'll head back to get things ready, then," she said with much less enthusiasm as she scooted ahead of us.

That lunch was hours ago, but my jaw still ached from chewing so much jerky. I must've eaten an entire dehydrated and shriveled-up cow, and my stomach still felt empty. "We're going to make a campfire after screen time," I told Sam. "Mr. Bosserman said something about making mountain pies, whatever they are."

"Sounds good." Sam yawned.

I opened my mouth to say, "Actually, it sounds horrible," but just then someone walked behind the screen of Sam's laptop. I couldn't make out the person, just his hand as it slapped down on Sam's shoulder. "Hey, man, you rocked it on the bars today. Killer amplitude!"

"Thanks, Tony," Sam said to the unseen boy. "See you back at the dorms."

"Killer amplitude?" I echoed.

"It's nothing," Sam said, but his grin told me otherwise. "Just kind of made a breakthrough on a move."

I bit back any complaint about Camp Paleo I was about to make. Here Sam had had an awesome day and now he had to listen to me whine. I nodded instead. "That's incredible!"

"So," he glanced at the corner of the screen, where it flashes the time, "I think we've only got a few minutes left. Tell me something awesome that happened to you today."

I swallowed, considering. Something good. That ruled out the sunburn peeling on my shoulders, the bug bite I got in my armpit, and the horrible broccoli-mixed-with-sauerkraut stench creeping from my rain-soaked sneakers. "Um," I considered, "Grandma and Mr. Bosserman have this flirty stuff going on."

A chuckle broke out of Sam again, so I told him all about Grandma and Mr. Bosserman and their plans for chow chow.

"It's pickled vegetables, like carrots and cauliflower," Sam said.

"How do you even . . ."

"My mom likes the stuff," Sam said. "She grew up in southern Pennsylvania, near there."

Mr. Bosserman's screen time stopwatch dinged.

"Five minutes, campers!" Jessica sang out.

Sam leaned forward, his face close to the screen. "Listen, Lucy," Sam said, his voice serious. "I know it's not your thing—you know—camping and fossil hunting and all of that. I know you're probably miserable and you're only there because I dared you to go. I feel really guilty—"

"Don't!" I interrupted, but he shook his head and put up his hand to silence me.

"But bringing your grandma and this Mr. Bosserman guy together, that's awesome! That's so . . . so you. You're great at that, pairing people up. I mean, look at us!"

Sam sucked in his breath. I think it's probably because of my face. I saw my expression in the corner of the screen when he said "us." My mouth had dropped open in a circle, and my eyes bulged. I forced my mouth shut with a pop.

"Uh . . ."

"I don't mean 'us' like we're a thing. Like a thing-thing. Just that you're good at bringing people together. Like packs." Sam's eyes were just as wide as mine. "I don't know why I'm talking so fast. Or why I'm still talking . . ."

"Time's up, camper wampers! Electronics off!"

"Bye," I said without really looking at Sam.

He just waved at me, mouth pressed shut, as I clicked on the hang-up button.

While we were having screen time, Mr. Bosserman and some of the counselors had set up about ten small fire pits next to the main camp area. The flames flickered high just as the sun was setting. The storm-cooled air and a nice breeze tickled the hair on my arms. I had to admit: it was beautiful here.

"Red up for dinner!" Mr. Bosserman called out, throwing up his wide hands like a crossing guard.

Jessica clapped and translated in her annoyingly chipper way, "Grab a plate, and start assembling your mountain pies."

Mountain pies, it turns out, were like pizzas. Woot woot! Take a slice of white bread, smother on some red sauce, add a fistful of shredded cheese and a sprinkling of pepperoni, and top with a second slice of bread. Then the whole contraption goes into this iron waffle maker–looking thing that presses it all together. Plunge it into the flames for about five minutes and *kazam*! Melty, drippy, delicious mountain pie!

The counselor who demonstrated mountain-pie making licked his fingers. The boy in front of me, Jer, flicked out his tongue like he could taste the greasy goodness.

Sheldon raised his hand as he spouted off, "I don't think cavemen would eat—"

Every single person at Camp Paleo snapped as one, "Shut up, Sheldon!"

Starving Camp Paleo campers rushed to the ingredients table, slapping together their mountain pies and dashing over to the fire. But my legs weren't moving as fast as they should. They, like the rest of me, were weighed down not just by the enormo hike we took earlier but also by Sam's words. About bringing people together being such a "me" thing to do. I wanted to find April and hear what she thought about what Sam had said.

Besides, it looked like April was searching for me, too. She stood on her tiptoes, scanning the line from the very back. I wiggled out of my spot to go to her. My arms waving, I rushed toward her. "Hey, April—"

"April! Over here!" Kira called from one of the fires. "I made you a mountain pie. It's just like mine. No disgusting pepperoni."

April flashed her split-your-face grin for just a second. "Extra cheese! Yay!"

Kira's eyebrow popped up. April took a deep breath. "I mean, that sounds awesome. Thank you!" She turned her grin into a good mimic of Kira's little half-your-mouth-tilts-up-slightly smile. "See you, Lucy," she said as she pranced toward Kira.

"But you love pepperoni!" I called.

April shook her head. "No, I always pick it off."

I guess she was right. I usually nabbed them off her plate. I had counted on doing it tonight, too.

Well, I might not have my friend, but at least I had mountain pie. I scooted back up to where I'd been in line. But everyone pressed closer together. All I saw were elbows! Someone—I think it was Amanda—even snarled at me.

Fine. I went to the end of the line, comforting myself that now I could take my time and make sure my mountain pie was perfect. And I did, spreading sauce over both slices of bread. Sprinkling cheese to each corner. Overlapping pepperoni perfectly across the top. This wasn't just any mountain pie. This was an LD (Lucy's Delight) Mountain Pie in the making. Sure, everyone else would be finished by the time I got my piping-hot pie of awesomeness out of the fire. But that was okay, because they'd all see me eating mountain-pie perfection as they dined on hasty regret.

I smooshed together the top and bottom pieces and handed it to Jessica. Only counselors were allowed to load the mountain-pie makers and shove them in the flames.

Just as she took the World's Greatest Mountain Pie from my hands, a lightning bolt shot across the sky. Thunder cracked so loudly and so close that Jessica jumped. My mountain pie landed on the ground with a thud. My poor mountain pie.

"No!" I gasped, and I swear, the word took at least ten seconds to get out.

"Oh, what a bummer!" chirped Jessica, still smiling. "Why don't you just scoot on over there and make yourself a new one?"

I huffed through my nose. My fists clenched and un-clenched. *It's okay*, I told myself. *Just make a new one.* And that's when the rain started. Not with a trickle but a waterfall. The fire gave up in a burst of grayish-black smoke and sizzling cries.

"Sorry, Lucy," Jessica sing-songed. "Looks like you're going to have a cold mountain pie."

I shivered under the leaky campsite roof, shoveling cold shredded cheese and sauce into my mouth and trying not to think of how no one in my pack, not even April, looked around for me before scurrying back to the bunks.

Only Mr. Bosserman waited with me, and he kept hurrying me along.

"Come on, come on," he said. "I've got to clean up after you and get back to my place, onest."

"To look for chow chow?" I asked.

His face flushed and he cleared his throat. "So, your, um, grandma. Does she like slippery pot pie with turkey or ham?"

"I don't even know what slippery pot pie is," I said, choking down a piece of soggy bread. "But if it's anything like mountain pie, I'd say she'd like it cooked."

The pattering of rain against the roof seemed to be a lullaby, making everyone fall asleep almost right away. Even Amanda's snoring was steady and even. April lay on her belly on the bunk above me. Her face was turned toward Kira's bunk like they had fallen asleep whispering. Which they had. April's long hair hung down over the side of the bed. I glared up at it, fighting the urge to yank it. Why was she spending so much time with other campers instead of me? And after all I had done for her this past year!

If it weren't for me, she wouldn't be in our pack at all. She'd still be sitting with just Sheldon at lunch every day. She'd still be a booger-eating no one. *I* was the one who told her she had to kick that disgusto habit! And this is the thanks I get: cold, lonely, mountain pie.

Amanda's snoring suddenly stopped, then kicked back in with a colossal snort. And her! She wouldn't be giving this meditation thing a shot if it weren't for me and Sam pointing out her anger issues all the time.

And Sheldon, he owed me massively, too. I was here, wasn't I? Even though Camp Paleo was the opposite of what I'd call a good time.

Where was the appreciation? We were supposed to be a pack! No one leaves the alpha wolf to eat cold mountain pie by herself!

I crossed my arms and grunted. Megan peeked over her covers. "Are you okay?" she whispered, completely proving my point. A complete stranger could ask me if I was okay while my pack ignored me.

I didn't answer, just rolled onto my side away from her. Soon I heard her breathing steady, joining the chorus of the others in the A-frame. Each of them slept peacefully while my stomach and feelings churned.

Slowly I drifted off, reminding myself that at least I had Sam. Maybe it was a good thing he wasn't at Camp Paleo. He'd be so disappointed in our pack, the way they had abandoned me. He'd remind them that I brought us all together, that bringing people together is what I'm good at doing.

That's it!

I sat up in a rush, bumping the top of my head on the bunk above me. April shifted but didn't wake. I smiled even though my head throbbed. *I'm good at bringing people together*. Sheldon, Amanda, and April just needed a reminder of that. April, especially. And what I needed to do was bring together the pack.

Just like Grandma and Mr. Bosserman possibly made a love connection through me, I'd show April and Sheldon they were meant to be. And, just like Grandma and Mr. Bosserman, a little love connection would make them easier to be around. Because if April was with Sheldon, then she'd really be connected to the pack. She'd stop trying to be like Miss I'm-too-cool-for-everyone Kira and go back to being April! The talking-in-bursts, happy-to-be-my-friend, up-for-anything-I'm-doing April!

Besides, I really did think April and Sheldon were meant to be—dorks in love! They just didn't know it yet.

This was going to be perfect. I bounced on my bed a little and realized I was clapping like a deranged Jessica.

"Ugh!" Kira's sleep-slurred voice echoed in our dark cabin. "I am surrounded by such losers! I am *trying* to sleep."

I stuck my tongue out at her, even though I knew she couldn't see, and lay back down. Now that I had a plan, I could sleep in peace. Annoying Kira had been a nice little perk, too.

My nose was hallucinating.

That's the only explanation for the savory scent of steak tickling my nostrils as I drifted off to sleep. I inhaled deeply. Yup. Definitely grilled, nondehydrated meat cutting through the smell of just-rained woods and mosquito repellent. I felt like one of those cartoon mice who smells cheese and floats toward the wedge with each breath. I didn't even realize I had climbed out of my bunk and wiggled into my flip-flops until I stepped off our creaky stoop and into the darkness.

I paused for a second as the wet grass tickled the sides of my feet. This was probably an enormously stupid idea. I mean, I know that Pennsylvania doesn't have wolves except for a few gated sanctuaries, but what about bears? Or mountain lions? I mean, weren't they the Penn State mascot? They probably were salivating for a juicy steak, too—or maybe fresh almost-twelve-year-old. I chewed my lip, considering if I should go through with this.

Plus there was the whole never-go-anywhere-by-yourself-or-else rule that Jessica had drummed into our heads without her usual perkiness on our first day. I glanced back at the A-frame. She was curled up like a kitten in her satiny pink sleeping bag.

I almost turned back to my bed. But then I heard, "Dang it, skeeters!" coming from the direction of the delicious aroma. I knew that voice.

I sneaked away from the cabin.

Chapter Six

I followed a little footpath as it snaked around the woods behind the main campsite. And there, on a patch of dry earth, stood the oddest thing. A caboose.

No joke! A caboose, like from the end of a train. It had a huge deck built around it with strands of lights hanging from the sides to light up the area around it. Even though it was pitch black outside, the lights illuminated our crotchety camp director. Mr. Bosserman stood behind a grill, flipping over the biggest, juiciest steak I had ever seen and swigging from a can of Coca-Cola!

"Cavemen do *not* drink Coke!" I hissed, stamping my foot on the deck stairs. "And they did *not* live in cabooses!"

"What in the—" For a second, I worried the oldy moldy would have a heart attack. He must've jumped a foot high at the sound of my outburst. Mr. Bosserman's hairy hand hovered over his heart. Then his eyes narrowed. "Why aren't you in bed, Missy?"

"I smelled food. Real, cooked, nonjerky food! And I'm starving."

Mr. Bosserman's mouth flopped open and closed six different times as he stared at me.

"Um, our steak is burning," I finally told him, pointing at the grill.

It took a lot of convincing, but Mr. Bosserman finally entered his caboose and brought out a plate for me. He kept going on and on about all the Camp Paleo rules I was breaking. But when I told him he'd be in even more trouble for letting me walk back to the cabin in the dark by myself, probably getting lost without the smell of steak to guide me, he said he'd march me back to my bunk.

"Great," I said. "But it'd be a shame to waste our steak. You know it's not any good warmed up."

Eventually, grumbling the whole time, he filled a plate with salad, half his baked potato, and a big chunk of steak. It wasn't exactly half, but I let that slide.

"You got any A-1 sauce?" I asked over a mouthful of buttery potato. "It's how steak is done."

Mr. Bosserman didn't even answer. He just glared.

"So, how'd you get this caboose?" I asked.

"My fool-headed son bought it for me, onest."

"What? Is he rich or something, to just go buying cabooses for people?"

"Rich enough to own this here camp. And Camp eMagine."

I almost spit out my steak. But then I came back to my senses and remembered this might be the last good meal I would have for another week and a half. I chewed slower. "Wait a sec! Your son, he's the owner of TechSquare? He's Alan Bridgeway?"

Mr. Bosserman's plastic patio chair squeaked as he shifted around. "Used to be Alan Bosserman, but he thought it sounded too bossy."

"I get that. Doesn't seem to bother you, though," I added.

Mr. Bosserman chuckled. "Alan always liked trains. 'Bout the only thing we had in common."

"Huh," I answered, shaking ranch dressing on my salad so it'd be edible.

Last year, when I was an absolute loner, I noticed the less I said, the more people talked. So it wasn't just the incredibly delicious food keeping me silent. I figured between the blanket of black sky, our filling bellies, and the awkwardness of the whole situation, Mr. Bosserman would fill in the blanks. And sure enough, he started talking. His words were spaced like pebbles being dropped into a lake, the ripples slowly overlapping.

Turns out, Mr. Bosserman and his son had spent a lot of time on trains. Every summer, all summer, in fact, starting when Alan was only five. They'd board a train with a suitcase each and just keep going until they saw the whole country.

"How'd you go a whole summer on a train? Didn't you get fired from your job?" I asked.

"I was a school janitor. Got summers off." Mr. Bosserman stood and picked up bottles of dressing and steak sauce. He made a grab for the salad bowl.

My hands darted out and grabbed the salad bowl from his hands. I shoveled more onto my plate and kept eating. "I'm not even close to being done yet," I said with a full mouth. "So, trains? How'd that start?"

He sighed and sat back down. "It was a bad year. The worst. My wife . . . well, she passed on. Cancer. She was a planner, Elise was. She had gone out and gotten a life insurance policy. When she knew . . . when we realized she wasn't . . . well, she made me promise I'd take some time for just me and Alan. Make sure that we were okay."

"I sort of get that," I said. "Sometimes things don't turn out how you planned. You have to make the most of what you've got, right?" I shook on some generic A-1 to sort of prove my point. "Bet Alan loved it."

Mr. Bosserman nodded. In the soft, orange glow of the stringed lights, I could see a small smile tugging at his mouth. "We did it up, best we could. We'd get off the train at different spots for a few days, find a campground, and spend the night under the stars. Just following the rails from campsite to campsite, making our own grub and livin' on the land. Once found a real dinosaur bone in Montana!

"But Alan, it was the engines that fascinated him. Had to know how they worked." He chuckled softly. "Always a mind for machines. By the time he got to high school, he had signed up for every tech summer class he could find."

After Alan discovered computers, Mr. Bosserman said, he didn't want to spend his summers on rails around the country. "I forced it for a while, making him go places with me. And if he wouldn't get on a train, I'd make him go camping with me around here. But his heart wasn't into it. Just made us both mad."

Mr. Bosserman rubbed at his bristly cheeks with his thick hand. "I always told him: got to learn from the past, too. Tried to get him to love nature as much as he loved pushing those dang computer buttons. Didn't think he got it, though. Not 'til he went and bought this camp. Can still hear him telling me about this place. Sounded like a little boy again."

"Did he make you Paleo's camp director right away?"

Mr. Bosserman rested his elbows on the table, facing out toward the woods instead of at me. "Nah. He bought all this land and made me promise to visit when I retired a couple years back. Finally, I did. He was fit to burst, so excited to show me around. First, all that fancy schmancy eMagine place." The way he said it, I knew the word "eMagine" tasted sour in his mouth. "Then he says, 'Look here at all this wooded area. Not sure what I'm going to do with it.'

"I says to him, 'Why not make an actual, real camp here? A fire-building, fossil-finding, honest-to-goodness camp for real kids?'" That chuckle sounded again. "Wasn't 'til later I realized he'd baited me, plain and simple. And like a fool minnow, I bit.

"'That's just what I'd hoped you'd say,' he had said. And he took me back here, to this caboose, told me I was director of Camp Paleo." Mr. Bosserman stood and gathered up the bottles of sauce and dressing, and this time I didn't say anything to stop him. "I'm the caretaker of the campgrounds in the winter, spring, and fall, director of Camp Paleo in the summer. Something to do." He shuffled back into the caboose. I could see when he opened the curved door that it had a little kitchen inside. I peeked into one of the round windows and saw a bed and a TV, too. The walls were lined with bookshelves, filled to overflowing.

"Do you live here year-round?" I asked when he returned, flashlight in hand.

"Yup. Fool-headed kid bought this caboose from the rail yard next town over. Trains stopped using cabooses in the 1980s. All these were rusting away. Just like Alan to find a new use for it. Spent more than this land's worth on cranes loading it up and gettin' it here. Then filling it with a kitchen and walls, outfittin' it with a bed. I daren't imagine how much that cost."

"He must really love you." My feet dragged as I followed him down the deck stairs. I closed my eyes, picturing my dad and our walks. How sad he would be when I was too old for them.

"Nah," Mr. Bosserman grumped. "Everything about me annoys him. Way I talk. Way I live. Just wants to keep me busy and outta the way."

"Seems like a lot of work to keep you out of the way. Wouldn't it be easier to put you in one of those old folks' homes?"

"I ain't that old!"

I shrugged, even though I bet it was too dark for him to see. "He must've liked trains a little to get a caboose."

"Fool-headed boy," Mr. Bosserman said again, but softer this time.

I followed just behind his steady steps, watching the flashlight's beam bounce along the pathway, my stomach full and happy, and my heart sad and homesick all at once.

Mr. Bosserman waited, keeping the flashlight steady into the A-frame, until I crawled under my covers. I glanced around. No one—not even my pack—had noticed I had snuck out.

❖ ❖ ❖

I slept in later than everyone else, only waking when a T-shirt was tossed into my face. I sat up and saw clothes everywhere, with more flying through the air. I rubbed my eyes. A sock smacked my cheek.

"I'm sure we'll find it," April was saying to Kira. "I mean, it couldn't have just walked off."

"Maybe you left it in the bathroom?" Megan suggested.

"What's going on?" I yawned.

"Ugh!" Kira threw a sweatshirt from the top bunk onto the floor with a soft thud. She was so mad that I could see little bits of spit fly from her mouth as she talked. "I remember putting my makeup bag right here in my duffel before we went on the hike yesterday. Right here!"

I climbed out of my bunk, tossing the T-shirt back on Kira's bed.

"You!" Kira yelled, pointing at me. "You took it, didn't you?"

"Now, now," Jessica said in her chipper way. "Let's not go blaming our friends!"

"We're not friends," Kira and I said in unison.

"I didn't take your stupid makeup bag." I stepped over a sweatshirt and got my own bathroom bag out of my suitcase. "Do I look like I wear makeup?"

I mean, seriously, I hadn't brushed my hair since we got to camp.

"It's a *designer* bag," Kira snapped. "Everyone would want it."

"Not me," Amanda said. I could almost mouth along when she added, "Designer labels make me angry."

"Besides," I said, "you were with me the whole day. When would I have snagged it? Face it. You just lost it."

"How do we know you didn't snag it when the rest of us were sleeping?" Kira yelled.

Megan sucked in her breath and stared hard at me. Guess maybe she might have noticed I had sneaked out last night. I turned away from her and back to Kira.

"I told you! I didn't take your stuff."

April zipped up her sleeping bag. "I'm sure it'll turn up eventually, Kira. You can go for the natural look until it does."

I rolled my eyes. The old April wouldn't have sounded so much like a magazine advice columnist.

"Where are you going?" Kira snapped as I threw back my sleeping bag cover and jumped to my feet.

"The bathroom!" I yelled back. "If it's okay with you, your highness!"

"Yeah, right," Kira muttered. "You're probably going to hide the evidence."

"Aargh!" I growled. I glared at April, waiting for her to tear into Kira on my behalf. But my so-called friend suddenly didn't seem to have anything to say.

I stomped out of the A-frame. When I got to the bathroom, I slammed the door as hard as I could, even though the A-frame was probably too far away to hear the forceful smack of wood against wood. The fat toad who lived in the bathroom seemed startled, though.

Chapter Seven

This sneaking away thing is addictive.

As we entered eMagine's computer lab, I heard Grandma's voice drifting out of the open cafeteria windows next door. "One serving of tater tots! One!" she yelled. "This isn't an endless buffet! Get your tots and move on."

As the rest of the Paleo campers walked into the lab, I crouched down and backed away.

"Where are you going?" Megan hissed.

"Don't worry about it," I said. "I'll be back in a minute."

"You better! You're going to get in trouble." She grabbed my wrist.

I shrugged her off and ducked out of the doors while perky Jessica pointed out empty lab seats. "I'll be right back!" I scanned the line, trying to make sure April, Amanda, and Sheldon wouldn't give me away. But April took a seat between Kira and Ash at the long table. And when Sheldon and Amanda passed me, they were already absorbed in which geology website to visit for tips on where to find the next fossil. They didn't even notice me.

I skidded into the cafeteria and almost blew my cover by standing there, mouth hanging open and staring at all the awesomeness. These campers were the exact opposite of cavemen in their gleaming cafeteria filled with screens, screens, and more screens. Television shows—oh, how I've missed you!—poured from monitors in each corner of the room. The brightly colored benches and tables held additional screens and even more were in the hands of the campers themselves. The kids buzzed to each other between bites of food, saying noncaveman-y things such as, "You're such a jimmy!" and "Stop rubber ducking and let's just do this!" One boy sitting alone just kept repeating, "Backdoor, backdoor."

"A jimmy?" I muttered.

"Someone who doesn't know what he or she is doing," a boy behind me said. He rolled his eyes but kept them on the tablet he held, not looking up at me at all. "It's what you call a person who doesn't know anything about programming."

"What's with the kid needing a backdoor?" I asked, thinking maybe he was another Camp Paleo stowaway.

The boy rubbed at his temples like I was such a jimmy. "It's something you put in so you can get to your program quickly for debugging."

"Debugging?"

The boy slowly backed away without answering.

In front of me, three girls sat with their knees on the cafeteria bench, elbows and foreheads touching, making the beads in their braided hair click as they crowded around an iPad. "Let's make the maze part harder. Maybe add a booster or something there," one said, making the girl next to her bounce a little.

"Yeah! Let's do this!" *Tap, tap, tap* on the screen.

"No! We should add a swerve here!" the third squealed.

I leaned over them, trying to see what they were doing. Seriously? They were creating an app. Not playing an app. *Making* one.

"Wow," I gasped. One of the three glanced up at me and widened her eyes.

The girl covered the laptop the way Sheldon covers the answers of his math quizzes so Tom can't copy him. "Let's add some refuctoring, pronto," she whispered. All three of them darted quick glances around the room, and then went back to programming.

The top half of the walls in the cafeteria were mirrored, making it look even more massive. And, unfortunately, forcing me to see myself.

I'll paint a little picture for you. Let's just say the only shower you've taken for the past few days has been standing under a trickle of cold water in a dark shower stall that had centipedes on the ceiling and baby toads by your feet. Maybe you forgot to bring in shampoo and so you just sort of scrubbed at your hair with soapy fingers. Let's say you couldn't bend over without your backside touching a slime wall so you hoped the suds would take care of the dirt coating your knees and your ankles. Then let's say that as soon as you left the shower stall, you immediately coated yourself in bug spray and sunscreen, which you've generously reapplied sixteen times since.

You might have forgotten to pack a hairbrush, so for the past three days, you've just shoved your hair into a ponytail and tried not to think about why your bangs weren't hanging across your forehead anymore. Turns out, that's because they stick straight out from your head in a stiff line. And let's say you forgot to change into your pajamas the night before and, since you were already dressed when you awoke, you just went with it.

Yup. I was looking pretty good . . .

I also was hungry, so I grabbed a tray and joined the lunch line. Judging from how the clean and sparkly eMagine campers in line scooted ahead, I'm guessing I smelled as fresh as I looked.

"Come on, come on, mealtime is almost over," Grandma muttered behind a tray full of fruit. She didn't look up.

I snickered. At least someone looked worse than I did. Grandma's frizzy hair was tucked into a bright yellow hair net, her hands covered in plastic gloves, and her face was cherry red and lined where sweat trickled down her cheeks.

A girl two spots ahead of me was stalling, staring at the different choices. I've got to admit, it was a bounty. There were fresh strawberries, sliced peaches, blueberries, and even some blackberries from which to choose. Grandma's ladle swayed over the options, following the girl's eyes as she scanned the fruit. Grandma still hadn't noticed me.

"Kid," asked Grandma, her voice hardening, "what's your favorite berry?"

"Barry?" the girl replied, eyes widening. "Um. Manilow, I guess."

"Manilow? That's way old school," the girl behind her scoffed.

"What can I say?" the first girl replied. "My folks are hipsters. And big Fanilows."

"Berry!" Grandma snapped. "Berry! As in *straw* or *blue*! Are you even *children*?" She whipped the ladle back and forth, making both girls back up. They shakily pointed to the peaches.

The girls scooted down the line to the more emotionally stable lunch ladies. "I'll take 'em all," I said to Grandma. "All the berries."

"'Bout time someone knows her mind," Grandma muttered and scooped fruit onto my tray without looking up. "Genius kids making me lose my mind . . ."

I coughed.

"Lucy!" she gasped, her eyes widening as she stared me in the face. "What are you doing here?"

"Good to see you, too, Grandma."

She ushered me behind the register to the big stainless steel kitchen, getting another lunch lady to take over the ladle for her. I held firm to my tray, snagging a ham sandwich on the way.

"What's up, Luc?" Grandma sat down on the steps outside the kitchen with a thump and dragged off her soggy hair net. Her hair puffed up like a mushroom.

I nibbled on the fruit and shrugged. "Just wondering how you are."

Grandma narrowed her eyes at me until I sighed.

"And maybe wondering some stuff."

"What kind of stuff?" Grandma slipped off her latex gloves and bunched them up into a ball. She tossed them toward a trashcan and fist pumped when they landed inside. "Sweet!"

I raised my eyebrows at her.

"What?" she snapped. "I've been picking up the lingo."

"Don't."

Grandma laughed. "All right. Spill. What stuff have you been wondering about?"

I pushed my now-empty tray off my knees and onto the step below us. "Love stuff."

"Dear Lord. Couldn't it wait until you got home?"

"No." I crossed my arms. "How do you make people fall in love?"

"You don't."

"That's it? I'm serious, Grandma," I said. "I know these two people. And they'd be great together. Really would solve a lot of problems if they just realized it, you know? So how do I make them realize it?"

Grandma stared at me a long time. She touched my bangs with a surprisingly gentle touch, stopped, and rubbed her fingers together. She patted my head instead. "Is this about me and Mr. Bosserman?"

"No!" I blurted. "Ew."

Grandma glared at me. "What do you mean 'ew'? I can't have romantic feelings?"

"Grandma!"

"Lucy!"

We stared at each other, both of our mouths opening and closing while we figured out what to say next. Pretty quickly I realized that going to my always-alone grandma for relationship advice might've been a poor choice. But her reaction did trigger a whole new set of questions.

"Where is Grandpa?"

"What?" This time, when Grandma shot to her feet, I couldn't tug her back down. She stared at me.

"I mean," I started, "I know how things work. If I've got a grandma, I've got to have a grandpa out there. Where is he?"

"Your mom never talked to you about this?"

I shrugged. I had asked Mom once where her dad lived. All she said is that she'd never met him. That he left Grandma before Mom had been born.

Grandma sighed. "Sometimes people think they're in love when they're not. Maybe what they really want is to not be alone anymore. Your so-called grandpa? He realized before I did that what we had wasn't love. He bailed out 'bout the same time I knew your mom was on the way."

"Well, he's a jerkface then." I crossed my arms. "You're lucky he left."

Grandma nodded, but didn't say anything for a moment. "Still would've been nice, you know. Not to be alone."

Suddenly my plot for April and Sheldon took a back-seat. Was my Grandma sad? "Do you still want that?" I asked quietly.

"Want what?"

"To not be alone anymore?"

"Nobody *wants* to be alone. Not really," she answered. Grandma put out her hand and I grasped it, letting her pull me up next to her. She kissed the top of my head, which was a pretty brave thing to do considering the state of my hair. "I wouldn't say *I'm* lonely. Not with you and your sister around."

"But Molly's in day care and I'm getting older . . ." I suddenly thought about Mr. Bosserman standing alone on his deck, saying his son was just trying to get him out of the way.

"Man, kid. Did you just come here to depress me?"

I pushed myself against Grandma's side. "No. I just . . . I think you should really give Mr. Bosserman a chance to share his chow chow."

Grandma laughed. "All right. I'll give him a chance."

"So, you really don't have any advice for me?" I pushed. "About getting two people to notice each other? Maybe even start to *like* each other?"

Grandma squeezed my shoulder. "I don't think so, Toots."

"What if they just don't realize how perfect they are for each other? What if someone points that out to them?"

"Someone like you?" Grandma asked, a furry eyebrow raised.

I shrugged.

"You can," Grandma said. "But when it comes down to it, whether two people hit it off will be up to them."

I made it back to the computer lab with twenty minutes of screen time left. "Told you I wouldn't get caught," I whispered to Megan as I took the empty seat behind her. She rolled her eyes at me and went back to typing furiously.

I pulled up the Camp Paleo blog and read the latest post, not wanting to wait for the breakfast printout.

Dear Super-Secret Camp Paleo Blogger:

Camp is great and all, but I've got bigger probs than tasteless jerky and soggy eggs. How do you tell a friend that you like her? I mean, like her.

From,

FossilFinder04

Dear FossilFinder04 and the rest of my fellow Paleo campers:

The only thing worse than a cold mountain pie is a lonely heart. Or, at least, that's what I've heard. As our esteemed leader would say, "Quit rutching and just tell her, onest!"

Put a group of us together, get rid of our parents, and make us survive on subpar nutrition and bug spray, and our hormones are bound to overreact. If you want my advice (and I'm not sure why you would, since you don't even know who I am), then just tell her.

We're all seeing connections that might or might not be real. Let's face it. The friends you make at camp probably aren't going to be lifelong buds. Neither are the friends you make at home, for that matter. Come on! We're barely tweens here! If you like her, say so. Camp should be a time for you to live the way you want to live, with nobody breathing down your neck about how to act or who to be.

Signing off,

Your SSCPB

FossilFinder04. Oh yeah, I think I know that boy. This was it! The nudge I needed to put Operation Dorks in Love in action. Clearly Sheldon, Camp Paleo's fossil finder, was talking about April. After all, he called her "a friend," which only leaves pack members. Since he's terrified of Amanda, that points to April. Score! Now I just needed to get April onboard.

Sam and I had decided to just email today since he had a late practice. I fired off a quick note about the day, but didn't mention Operation Dorks in Love.

For some reason, my fingers couldn't even type the word *love* in a message to Sam.

Chapter Eight

Major drama at the excavation site!

After our usual gritty egg and watered-down orange juice breakfast, we headed back to look for more fossils. I heard Sheldon's teeth grind together as we made our way toward the dig site. The spot where Sheldon had uncovered his leaf fossil days earlier was swarmed with digging campers. Next to Sheldon, Amanda cracked her knuckles. Maybe she needed an extra dose of morning meditation. Amanda looked ready to plow over the campers huddling where Sheldon first found a fossil. "Come on," she eventually said through clenched teeth. "Let's find fresh ground."

Sheldon and Amanda headed down a little incline and completely complicated my master plan. Because smack dab in the middle of the campers swarming Sheldon's former dig site was Kira. Next to Kira stood April, laughing at those lame robot dance moves Kira's twin brother, Ash, was making.

I tapped April on the shoulder when she was still mid-laugh. She turned, eyes sparkling and smile wide, though it shook a little when she saw it was me. "Come over this way," I said. "The pack's onto a new site."

"Oh! Um." She looked toward Kira and Ash, who both watched us.

"Yeah, maybe if she wanted to hang out with a bunch of geeks." Kira rolled her eyes. "We'll stay here, thanks."

I half-laughed, half-grunted. "We're not geeks, right April?" I nudged her with my elbow. "We're dorks."

Megan, who was close by, laughed, but Ash and Kira just stared at me.

"That was a joke," I offered.

Blank stares.

"Okay," I said slowly, turning back to April. "Are you joining us, or what?"

April chewed her bottom lip and looked again toward the twins. Kira rolled her eyes again, making it really hard not to whap her in the back. Dad once told me not to make stupid faces because if someone hit me hard on the back, I'd be stuck with that face forever. Ash's eyes swept over me, like he knew what I was thinking.

"Let's give it a shot," he finally said.

"Are you serious?" Kira gasped.

He shrugged, his smile spreading at his sister's outrage. "They found the first fossil in camp. Maybe they're onto something."

"Whatever," Kira said, again turning her back to us. "April and I are staying here."

Ash and I both turned to April. "You could come with us, April," Ash prompted.

I had never seen my friend so unsure. April usually plowed into things, kicking the blocker in karate until the tops of her feet bruised, skipping down the street without worrying once about how her arms flailed, and howling like a wolf in a full cafeteria. But now she stood in front of me, her hair slicked into braids like Kira's.

Her eyes boring into Ash's like she was trying to read his mind. Worrying her lip instead of spouting out an answer. Where was my April? Pack April? She smiled, and suddenly I saw her.

"Sure! Let's go!" But then, after a deep breath, she added, "This place looks pretty picked over anyway."

"Awesome!" Ash said, then turned to the boy beside Kira. "How about you, Jer?"

Jer, who shared Sheldon and Ash's A-frame, kicked a hacky sack and popped it up to his knee, then knocked it to his other ankle and back up again to the other knee. Over and over. The four of us—Ash, April, Megan, and I—watched the little ball whip around. I had to admit, I had still sort of been avoiding this kid. Partly it was be-cause whenever he saw me, Jer waved like crazy at me the way he thought I had when we met the first day. He also winked at me whenever we passed. I wasn't sure if it was deliberate. Maybe he had some sort of eye twitch or something. But also, as someone who is first out in dodgeball, misses every serve in volleyball, and whose only score in basketball was for the other team, I'm not naturally drawn to super athletes (secretly incredible gymnasts, aside).

And Jer always had a ball in his hands. Seriously! When he got to camp his backpack was bulging with a basketball, which Mr. Bosserman confiscated. ("Cavemen didn't play basketball!") Next time I saw him, he was pounding a tennis ball against the A-frame. Mr. Bosserman took that ball, too.

Megan's arm brushed mine as she stepped forward, her eyes following the hacky sack until Jer bounced it on his forehead. Then her eyes stayed on his face. I squinted, trying to see what had captured her attention. I guess he was kind of cute; he had dark skin and greenish blue eyes and was about three inches taller than even April. He hit the ball with his heel and head butted it again. Hmm. If Jer realized Megan was into him, maybe he'd stop all the winking.

"He's pretty cute, huh?" I whispered to Megan.

"Mega cuteness," Megan whispered.

Jer kept bouncing around the ball, doing a few more tricks now that he had us as an audience.

"You know Mr. Bosserman is just going to take that from you, right?" I pointed out.

Jer tapped the ball toward me with his ankle. I stepped aside. Megan's thin little hand shot out and grabbed it.

"Wow, nice catch!" Jer said, his hand open for it to be tossed back. Megan's face flushed pink and her fist closed around the ball. Again Jer held out his hand.

I nudged Megan, who seemed to have forgotten English. "He wants the ball back."

She nodded and held out her hand. Jer tugged at the ball, and we all sighed when she finally let go.

"Ah, look," Kira said in her snotty way. "The geek's in love with you, Jer!"

"Shut up!" Ash and I shouted at the same time.

Next to me, Megan squeaked. That's really the only way to describe it. She squeaked like a tiny frog. Tears burst out of her eyes as she rushed away.

Kira laughed, even though Ash told her to shut up again. She rolled her eyes. I think it might be the only facial expression she can make. "Jerk much?" I snapped at Kira, who just rolled her eyes.

"Let's go," Ash muttered. We walked toward Sheldon and Amanda and past Mr. Bosserman. Even though Jer kept going with the hacky sack, the old grump didn't take it away. He even grunted at a pretty spectacular ankle-to-knee-to-other-ankle-to-head-butt action.

"He's in a weirdly good mood," April said in her new careful way.

I just nodded, not ready to talk to her after she didn't stick up for Megan with me. If she *had* stuck up for Megan—or even been a little more Aprilish—I would've told her about the laughter I heard tickling the air last night from the general direction of a certain caboose. I'm pretty sure it was Grandma's chuckle.

I tried some of Amanda's deep breath *kumbayas* to curb my anger at April as we made our way toward Sheldon and Amanda. It's not like I can't relate to doing mean things because I wanted someone to like me. I pretty much did that my whole fourth-grade year up until I ditched Becky and Tom to hang out with Sam. (Honesty alert: *They* ditched me. But I prefer to think of it the other way around, and when Sheldon invents the time machine to go back and check out real dinosaurs, I'm going to have him drop me off at the beginning of fourth grade and do the ditching myself.)

Surprisingly, the deep breaths and *kumbayas* helped, and I was back to Operation Dorks in Love. "Look!" I pointed to a spot beside Sheldon and Amanda. "There's a perfect place for you right there." I half-pushed, half-dragged April to the little crevice between Sheldon and the embankment.

"Hey, April!" Sheldon said. His grin stretched so far that if it reached another inch, his ears would be turning upward, too.

Next to me, Ash made a coughing noise.

"What?" I asked.

"Um, you're twisting your fingers together like a mega-villain. That's all."

I shrugged. "Just getting ready for fossil hunting." I tried to sound casual as I made my way to a spot on the other side of Amanda. Her hands raked the dirt, sending clumps flying like my neighbor's Rottweiler. The hard-packed dirt and rocks left behind were then carefully checked out by Sheldon, who piled everything behind him.

"Villains are cool," Jer said. "But I prefer superheroes. Who's your favorite?"

Megan sat on the top of the embankment, her face in her hands, but I knew she was listening to us. Maybe I could do a third matchup. "I don't like superheroes," I said, even though it's a total lie. "But I think Megan does. Don't you, Meg?"

The only response was a little tip forward and back of her black hair.

"Cool," Jer said.

"What do you mean you don't like superheroes?" Amanda grunted.

"Yeah," said Sheldon, wiping his fingers on his khaki shorts. The dirt just trickled down to stick to the ever-growing stain on his pulled-up tube socks. "You made us all pick our favorite Avenger. You made me Hulk." He growled and flexed his muscles, making the vein in his neck pop out.

"I still think I should've been Hulk," Amanda muttered. "You wouldn't like me when I'm angry."

"You're always angry," I snapped.

"That's my secret." She smiled.

"You're Thor. Sam is obviously Captain America. April is Black Widow, and I'm Nick Fury," I told them.

"I thought you were Black Widow." Sheldon said.

"Now I'm Nick Fury," I snapped.

The two of them finally went back to digging. I climbed to sit next to Megan. She twisted a silver bracelet in circles around her wrist. "You can be Iron Man," I whispered. She shrugged but didn't turn away.

And that's when mega drama broke out!

"I think I found something!" Ash said, peering at a chunk of dirt and rock in the dig site. He blew off some of the dirt around it.

Sheldon rushed forward. "OMG! OMG!" (He said it just that way, letters only.)

"What?" April asked.

Amanda barged forward and knelt next to Sheldon. Ash slowly stood and backed away from Sheldon, Amanda, and whatever he had discovered.

"Is that what I think it is?" Amanda asked.

"Yes!" Sheldon screamed. He pulled up the flat rock and cradled it in his palm.

Together, he and Amanda yelled, "A complete trilobite!"

"A what?" Jer asked, momentarily not throwing his hacky sack in the air.

In an awed voice, Sheldon continued, "Oh, nothing. JUST THE FIRST ORGANISM TO HAVE EYES!"

"Boom!" Amanda wiggled her hips in a little jig. "A genuine *Phacops rana.*"

"When did you start speaking Sheldon?" I could see the funny-looking fossil from our perch on the embankment. If you mushed the body parts of a crab with a shrimp and added marble eyes, that's what a trilobite looks like.

Amanda kept dancing. "Hobbies like archeology are great for anger management!" Wiggle, wiggle, wiggle.

I thought for a second that Sheldon's excitement had led to a seizure, but that's just how he danced.

"What's the big deal?" Ash asked.

"It's like seven hundred million years old," Amanda snapped. "That's what!"

Quietly, Sheldon corrected her. "Five hundred or so at the oldest. More likely three hundred fifty million years old."

"Wow," Ash said, leaning in to look at the fossil as Jer darted back up the hill to where the other campers were digging.

"Guys! Ash found a fossil a thousand million years old!" Jer shouted.

Paleo campers barreled down the hill like a herd of buffalo. Sheldon cradled the trilobite Ash had found to his chest, muttering random facts like Amanda's *kumbaya* chant and protecting it from the crowd. "Pennsylvania state fossil. Fairly common. Usually found in pieces. Devonian age."

Sheldon backed up, pressed against the embankment, eyes squeezed shut as the campers rushed him.

"Let me see it!"

"Can I hold it?"

"Where'd you find it?"

Mr. Bosserman tried to wrangle toward the front of the crowd, but no one let him by, even though he was yelling so loudly his nose turned purple. Jessica stood beside him, clapping her hands like she was calling puppies.

One voice rose above the others. My nemesis, of course. "Why are you holding it, geek? Jer said my *brother* found the fossil!" Kira put out her hand for the fossil, the other hand on her hip.

Sheldon now curved over the trilobite like a comma. He was shaking his head and still muttering in full-out panic mode. If anyone tried to get the trilobite from him, they'd have to pry back his fingers one by one.

"He can have it," Ash said. "I don't care." Ash backed off, his hands up.

I wanted to do something to stop Sheldon's panic—his fact chant kept getting shriller and shriller—but no one listened as I yelled for everyone to give him space.

"Cambrian period possibility. World's largest found in Canada. Native American amulets . . ." Sheldon's neck vein bulged and his knuckles turned white around the trilobite. He was about to go Hulk.

Amanda spit out *kumbayas* as quick as Sheldon's monologue of facts.

Then Kira made a grab for the fossil, and that's when everything erupted.

Amanda leaped in front of Sheldon with ninja grace. Her hands splayed and arms up, she yelled so loudly and deeply that spittle flew into Kira's cocky little face. "BACK! OFF!"

Total silence from Camp Paleo. Even the mosquitos stopped buzzing. Amanda took a heavy, stomping step forward, and every single Paleo camper took a step back. "You are in an evacuation zone!"

Quietly Sheldon corrected her. "Excavation zone." I was glad to see his fingers relax slightly.

"Everyone needs to BACK OFF!" Another step forward from Amanda, another herdlike step back from the campers. This continued until everyone was off the little hill.

"Well, it's not like you can keep it," said Kira, arms crossed at the edge of the dig. "It belongs to the camp."

"Nah, you can keep it," Mr. Bosserman said. "Finder's keepers." He sort of whistled as he walked back up the hill.

Remembering my mission, I nudged April. "Go congratulate your boy!" I said to her.

April's eyes widened and her face flushed deep red. "You think I should?"

"Absolutely!" I clapped, then thought of Jessica and quickly stopped.

"Okay!" April breathed. "I will! I am! I'm going to congratulate!"

"Yes!" I cheered. "Congratulate!" (Like I said, April Speak can be contagious.)

But then, oddly, April went right past Sheldon and went up to Ash. Ash!

My head swiveled over to Sheldon. His eyes were locked on the back of Amanda, who was Rottweilering through more mounds of dirt. And the look on his face? It was the expression he usually reserved for dino nuggets. "You can be Hulk from now on," he breathed to Amanda.

"Thanks." Amanda grinned back, their eyes locking.

Lollipop farts!

"So." I jumped, startled by the voice at my side. "You want to excavate with me?" Jer stood beside me, balancing his hacky sack on the tips of two fingers.

"Uh . . ."

"Come on," Jer said. He leaned closer to me, so I could see the way his thick eyelashes tangled. "I think I already found my treasure." He chuckled and then—horror of horrors—he winked at me. Behind me, Megan squeaked again.

"Is someone putting you up to this?" I asked. I mean, seriously, he winked.

"No." The hacky sack dropped to the ground with a thud. "I was catching all sorts of vibes from you."

"Not me!" I said. "From Megan!"

I thrust my thumb back toward where Megan sat, face covered, squeaks sounding.

"But—"

I pushed past Jer, past Sheldon staring at Amanda, past April giggling at Ash, past Mr. Bosserman whistling, and headed toward Camp eMagine.

I had to get out of there before my matchmaking powers mutated again and more of the wrong people fell in love.

Chapter Nine

What a disaster! The pack was doomed.

Sheldon's feelings for Amanda had to fade fast. She was too tough to be all lovey-dovey. I figured we'd lose one of them from the pack due to the massive awkwardness. And April, falling for stupid jerkface Ash! (Okay, I'll admit, Ash isn't really a jerk. He's actually pretty nice. But he's a twin with Queen Jerkface of Kingdom Snob.) If she started spending all of her time with Ash and Kira, I'd never get my old reliable April back again.

Add to this, my only new recruit, Megan, hated me because Jer got the stupid idea I liked him. Seriously! Does he have a ping-pong ball for a brain? What could possibly make him think I liked him?

Of course, I did smile at him a lot today. But only to encourage Megan! Megan! And, okay, so he was watching while Megan and I whispered about him. But Megan whispered; I listened!

"Ugh. This is such a disaster!" I slumped on the stoop outside the eMagine kitchen, where I'd run to spill all my problems out to Grandma.

"Earthquakes are disasters. Tornados and wildfires, too." Grandma chomped on her nicotine gum. Camp eMagine wouldn't let anyone, even cranky old lunch ladies, smoke, so Mom had sent her a care package of gum that's supposed to make her stop wanting to smoke.

Guess what was in my care package? Nothing, that's what. Because I never even got a care package. Why does Grandma get a care package but not me? I don't know.

"I don't know anything." I muttered.

Grandma sighed. "You know nothing about love, that's for sure."

"Thanks," I snapped.

"Well, you can't just decide who should partner up and expect it work."

"Yes, I can. I'm good at pulling people together," I said, pushing out my bottom lip in a small pout.

Grandma shrugged and blew a giant bubble. She must've had six pieces of gum in her mouth to make such a huge bubble. "Maybe," she said. "But when you brought your so-called pack together, you weren't really trying. You were just being you. You were being *kind*."

I glared at her. "I *am* kind!"

She snorted, then glanced at her watch. I guess I had to get back to camp, but I wasn't ready to face anyone. In the distance, I heard a quick three claps, followed up with a high-pitched, "Lucy! Lucy, you get back here right now!" *Clap-clap-clap.*

Crap sandwich. Jessica was on to me.

"Grandma," I asked, "if you had to run away, how would you do it?"

Grandma spit her gum into a napkin and crossed her arms. "My guess would be that you'd need to get a lot of cash, change your appearance, and, most of all, not contact anyone you know. I'd give it a lot of thought before I attempted it. And be sure to pick someplace warm. A beach or island."

I stared at her.

"What?" she asked, unwrapping another piece of gum.

"That was just unexpectedly specific." Jessica's claps got closer. "I didn't think you'd actually give me steps to follow."

"Well, maybe I had to think about it once."

Clap! Clap! Clap! "Lucy!" Jessica was almost there.

I stood on the stoop. "Can I at least have a cookie before I go?"

"What do I look like?" Grandma snapped. I let my eyes deliberately run up and down her aproned, hair-netted, plastic-gloved body.

She stomped inside and thrust a chocolate chip cookie out of the door. "Don't run away," she snapped.

"Now, we've been over these rules, Lucy," Jessica said as we walked back to the Camp Paleo dig. "And, wouldn't you agree, there aren't that many rules? Just three teeny, tiny rules. That's all."

I nodded, but she prattled on anyway.

"One: Brush your teeth every day. Two: Help prepare meals when it's your day. Three: Don't wander off." Jessica said the last one extra loud.

"Got it," I said. "Sorry."

In her high-pitched, sing-songy voice, Jessica said, "I'm afraid sorry doesn't cut it."

"What does that mean?"

"Well, the thing is, number three is our biggest rule of all." She smiled brightly. "The one with consequences." She mimed a super sad face. "Someone's going to miss tonight's activity!"

I struggled not to smile and to keep my fist pump mental. "Guess no hike for me! You know, I was so bad, you should force me not to go on the fossil dig tomorrow, too."

Jessica giggled and patted my head. For real. Like I was a dog. "We're not hiking, tonight, sweetie. Tonight we're swimming!"

"What?"

"Yes, we're swimming in Lake Matilda tonight. Everyone is changing into their swimsuits now, but I guess you're fine the way you are."

She tilted her head then and looked at me with narrowed eyes. I glanced at my dirt-encrusted self. For a bitter second, I let myself think about what it would feel like to have cool water wash the grime from my hair, the mud from my knees, and the sticky bug spray from my skin.

Jessica must've had the same thought. "Of course, while they're changing, you could take a shower." Her nose wrinkled. "Maybe a nice, long one."

My life stinks.

Jessica might not be my favorite person, but I could've hugged her after taking a shower. It felt so nice to see mini rivers of muddy water run down my legs and down the drain. The centipede and I seemed to have reached an agreement: I wouldn't try to crush him with my feet and he'd keep his thousand legs away from me. At the end of my shower, I felt so much better that I decided to give him a nice refreshing splash. He had to be roasting on the cement floor! But that only made him float down the drain. Oops.

And this time, I even remembered the shampoo and clean underwear!

But after my shower, I felt like a dirtball all over again. Only this time, the feeling came from the inside.

Everyone in the A-frame quieted as I walked in. I thought at first they were in awe of my cleanliness. But then I realized—nope. They'd been talking about me. All it took was one glance at Kira, gloating on the top bunk in her purple ruffled bikini, to realize it. Megan, in a rainbow tank, wouldn't look at me. And April? She feverishly applied sunscreen, even though it was five o'clock at night.

"What's up?" I decided to just play it off like I didn't care.

"They're all talking about you," Amanda said. She wore a camo swimsuit and an enormous smile.

"Amanda!" April gasped.

"Why are you happy about them talking about me?" I snapped to Amanda. "Shouldn't that make you angry?"

"It does," Amanda said, still smiling. "But I can't stop being happy today. It's weird."

"What did you guys say about me?" I crossed my arms and glared at April and Kira.

Still smiling, Amanda answered instead. "Kira says you're a drama queen, running off like that."

In a small voice, April added, "I told her you just missed your grandma. That's all."

Kira snickered. In a baby voice, she added, "Poor little girl misses her mommy, too, I bet. And maybe her blankie-wankie."

Amanda snickered. "That's funny. It's like she knows about Mr. Stinky."

My eyes filled with water as Kira bellowed. Even Megan laughed a little. I squeezed my eyes shut so the water wouldn't spill over. The thing is, I know Amanda wasn't trying to poke fun at the stuffed bear I had since I was baby. She went right back to humming "ommm" and folding her beach towel. She was just being Amanda, a little clueless about feelings but generally a good friend. A good friend who was—what? Putting on lip gloss? I shook my head and looked away. Kira laughed again.

Kira just twisted everything. She was ruining my whole pack, especially April, who simply sat down on her bunk and didn't look at me.

And suddenly I felt grimy.

Later, sitting by the side of the lake, I thought of a million things I should've said to Kira. But really, she was sort of right. I do miss Mom. Dad, too. And Molly, even if she has become a werebaby. And, yeah, I miss Mr. Stinky.

I let my eyes wander over to where Kira stood knee-deep in the lake. She was talking to some girls from a different A-frame. Then they all bent over, laughing. They turned toward me. Kira flipped her hair off her shoulder, making the setting sun shimmer on her long locks, and turned her back to me. I looked down at my scabby knees, the bug bites clustered on my thighs, and the peeling skin on my shoulders from my healing sunburn.

When I looked back at her, she and the other girls were whispering and pointing toward a cluster of boys splashing a little deeper in the lake. They'd pop up like dolphins and pull down the guy closest to them. Someone said their older brother went to camp here a few years back and a fish chewed off his nipple. Now the boys were daring each other to go farther out.

After a while, the boys stopped worrying about nipple-eating fish and concentrated on sneaky splash attacks on the girls. It was just a game, but somehow more, too. Too much showing off and a lot of loud laughing.

I felt so small, suddenly. I mean, I know Kira is going into fifth grade, like me. But somehow, I still was a little girl and she looked and acted like my teenage babysitter.

On the shoreline, Amanda showed Sheldon yoga moves she had learned during meditation sessions that morning. They stretched out into warrior poses. Sheldon's thin, pale arms looked like shadows of Amanda's thick, muscly moves. In unison, they moved into a tree pose. Sheldon's face shined, and I don't think it had to do with the sun's reflection.

Even Amanda and Sheldon were more mature than me.

I had to get better at this. I had got to stop being a little girl and start being an almost teen, too.

I let my thoughts scatter as Megan plopped down beside me. "I heard you aren't allowed to swim," she said quietly.

"I wouldn't have taken my chances with the nerple-eating fish anyway."

"Nerple?" she asked.

I shrugged. "I have trouble saying the other word."

"Nipple?"

I shuddered.

"You can't just change the word because you don't like it," Megan said.

"I just did."

Megan stood.

"Hold on!" I pulled her back down. "I'm sorry. I'm just really grouchy. And I'm sorry, too, about the whole Jer thing. I know you like him."

Megan twisted her body around and I followed her gaze to where Jer skipped rocks across Lake Matilda. He rocked up on his heels every time the rock hit the surface of the water and went back for another arc.

Megan leaned back on her elbows. "Thanks, but if he doesn't like me, what can I do about it?" Megan smiled, revealing small, straight, super white teeth. "He's just really *bouncy*, you know? If you like him, you should tell him. I won't be upset or anything."

I shook my head. "I don't like him."

"So who *do* you like?" Megan asked.

For some stupid reason, Sam's face popped in my head. The way he looked on the screen when he said "us."

"No one," I said. "I mean, I don't like anyone here."

I scanned the lake again. Sheldon and Amanda were twisted in a strange yoga pose I'm pretty sure one of them had just made up. Each had a leg straight up in the air, one arm twisted behind and the other arm locked behind. They were like straight-legged pretzels.

Two kids snuck up behind them and pushed them at the same time in the middle of the back, making both fall over. April was between them and the lake, talking to Ash, and she just let the jerks run right by her. I know from watching her spar in tae kwon do that she could've taken them down with one well-placed flying sidekick. But she didn't even look up. It's like the three of them didn't even know each other! I guess April was too caught up in Ash to notice.

Sheldon popped up before Amanda and tore off after the kids, Amanda just behind him, urging him to calm down. Amanda! Telling someone to calm down!

The pack was completely falling apart! I had to do something a-sap!

Maybe the first mission in Operation Dorks in Love had failed, but phase two was going to rectify this damage. I had to get April back to her senses, away from Kira and Ash, and back to the pack. Then I'd deal with Sheldon and Amanda, if needed. (They actually were kind of cute together.)

"It's too bad you don't like Jer," Megan said. I had to concentrate to remember what we were talking about. "Because he's on his way over here, and I'm pretty sure it's to talk to you, not me." I looked over and, sure enough, there he was, bouncing toward us. Something about that, the way he punctuated every move with a little bounce, reminded me of April. The real April. The way she used to be.

I smiled.

"Why are you doing that twisty thing with your fingers again?" Megan asked.

"Phase two, about to commence."

"Ooo-kay," Megan said slowly. "I'm going to swim. Good luck."

"Hey, Megan," I called to her. "What do you think of Ash?"

"Kira's brother?"

"Yeah," I said. "I think he likes you."

Chapter Ten

Jer plopped down beside me in the spot Megan had just left. He leaned back on one elbow and smiled. "You afraid to swim? I'll keep you safe from the fish." Another wink.

"Do you have an eye twitch?" I asked.

He squirmed. You know how sometimes you get a flash of insight into a person? Like you see someone smiling, but you know it's a total fake and that he's really sad? Or you see someone trying to look cool but you know she's really bursting with happiness inside? Well, I got a little flash from Jer's squirm. Jer was as awkward and freaked out about this whole romance thing as me. I had a feeling all he really liked was playing sports. He flirted because everyone else was doing it. Suddenly I liked him a lot more. Not *like* like him. You know what I mean.

"Never mind. Look, I have a boyfriend." I lie so easily sometimes. "You don't know him."

"What's his name?"

Not Sam. Not Sam. "Huh?"

"His name?"

Not Sam. Not Sam. "Ham."

"Your boyfriend's name is Ham?" Jer cocked his head at me.

"It's a nickname. And no one knows about him, so don't go running your mouth. Look, that's not important. The thing that's important is that I'm not interested."

"Whatever." Jer rolled a pebble around in his hand and started tossing it back and forth. "Not like I care."

"Right," I said, rolling my eyes until I remembered Kira always does that. I stopped mid-roll. "Anyway, *I'm* not interested, but I know someone who does like you. A lot."

This got Jer's attention. He dropped the pebble. "Who?"

"April."

❖ ❖ ❖

Jer sat up and squinted across the shore toward where April and Ash were talking. April laughed at whatever Ash was saying. "Seems like she's pretty into Ash," Captain Obvious said.

"You're the one she talks about all the time," I lied again. I had my fingers crossed, but still felt guilty. *It's for the good of the pack,* I told myself.

"Yeah?" Jer nodded, his bottom lip popping out a little. "I thought I got a vibe from her."

"You totally did. She's been hanging around Ash to find out more about you. Since you're friends with him."

Jer's chest puffed out a little. "Makes sense. She's pretty smart, huh?"

"Super smart," I said. "And she has a total thing for athletic guys. Like you. She loves—*loves*—sports."

"Like what?"

"Oh, you know. Football, soccer, hockey." Honesty alert: April hates all team sports. I've heard the best lies have a little bit of truth mixed in, so I listed some individual sports, too. "Um, karate, track. She wants to get into juggling. All the sports."

"Huh." Jer got up, brushing the sand off his shorts.

"One more thing." I jumped to my feet and grabbed his arm before he could strut over to April and ruin everything. "She's really shy. So it's tough for her to say she likes someone. But she's really into you, even if she might not seem like it all the time."

"Hard to get, huh?" Jer smoothed his hair with his hands. "I can handle that."

"And, um, she'd kill me if she knew I told you. So don't say anything, cool?"

"Cool." Jer stretched and grinned at me. "The coolest girl at camp, and she likes me." He did a little fist pump and headed toward April. Soon he was next to her, trying to teach her how to skip rocks. She dived into the lake and swam away from him. Jer gave me a thumbs up and paddled after her.

April? The coolest girl at camp? Ha! I laughed so hard I couldn't breathe.

"Freak!" a kid muttered as he passed me.

❖ ❖ ❖

Today's post from your Friendly Super-Secret Camp Paleo Blogger is brought to you by the letter L. That's right: L as in Love. What's with all the hook-ups going on around Camp Paleo? As our esteemed leader would say, "Cavemen didn't flirt, onest!"

It's like way back in first grade, when someone has a birthday party at that clown pizza place. Suddenly that's where everyone has a party, even though clowns are creepy and the pizza tastes like play dough. Here we are, where two people crush on each other and suddenly the whole camp is pairing off.

As we move into our second and final week of Camp Paleo, let's remember the real reason we're here: figuring out what we like about ourselves. That's right, ourselves. You're missing your chance, lovesick campers! Let me remind you, we all go home at the end of the week. Maybe you'll exchange email addresses, but the only person you can count on seeing again is the face in the mirror.

Take this week and figure out who you want that person to be. And then be him or her.

Signing off,

SSCPB

P.S. If someone says she just not into you that way,
BELIEVE HER.

"Definitely a girl," Sheldon said later that night during screen time.

"Definitely." Amanda and Sheldon shared one station at the lab, heads tilted toward each other as they watched the screen. Sheldon operated the keyboard, Amanda the mouse. She clicked off the Camp Paleo homepage and Sheldon typed in the address for a trilobite message board.

"Wait!" Sheldon snapped. "This guy says his trilobite is better than ours because it's bigger. But ours is intact. Aargh! Them's fighting words!"

"*Kumbaya*. He just doesn't know, Shel." Amanda twirled something hanging from her neck.

I leaned in for a better look and screamed. "Amanda! There's something on you!"

"Oh, this?" She held up her trilobite necklace. "Sheldon made it. He threaded the string right through the eye socket hole."

Sheldon, looking up from the message board, said, "American Indians used to make fossil amulets all the time."

I threw up a little in my mouth as they stared into each other's eyes.

My computer pinged with an incoming Skype call. I sucked in my breath, deciding if I wanted to answer Sam's call. He'd be so mad about me lying to Jer about April. But, just as quick, I was the angry one. If he had been here like he had promised, none of this—none!—would've happened. We'd be having the best summer ever, just like I had planned.

So I took the call. "Hey, Sam."

"Hey!" He smiled hugely, taking me by surprise. For most of the time I've known Sam, his smiles are super slow, starting in his eyes and then sometimes getting to his lips, but not always.

"Why are you so happy?"

His smile faltered a little then, going back to its usual size. "No reason. Just had a good day. How about you? How's living like a caveman?"

I shrugged, having a hard time meeting his eyes. "It's all right."

"What's going on, Lucy?"

"Hey, Sam!" Sheldon and Amanda leaned into my screen. Then the two of them left the computer lab.

Sam's mouth dropped open and he suddenly looked a little pale. "Are they—were they *holding hands*?"

I nodded. "You just met Shemanda." Then I filled Sam in on how Amanda saved the trilobite.

"And stole Sheldon's heart. Wow." Sam shook his head. "I never would've thought. Sheldon and April, maybe . . ."

"I know!" I thumped the desk. "Exactly!"

"I guess that means you and April have been hanging out a lot." I could tell Sam was fishing, trying to figure out why I was acting distant. And, all right, maybe he was making sure I was okay—that all of our friends were okay.

"Nope." I shifted in my seat. "Her parents got her a laptop before camp started, so she's at a table in the back of the room."

"I didn't mean now, like literally during screen time. I mean all the time," Sam said.

"Look, we only have another minute of screen time and I've still got to email my mom and dad, so . . ."

"Lucy?"

"Bye, Sam." *Click.*

I read an email from Mom and Dad, which included a picture of Molly sitting up all by herself, and started to write back. But I ended up just writing, Miss you.

I wrote to SSCPB instead.

Dear SSCPB:

Is it ever okay to lie? What if you're doing it to help your friends?

Please answer,

PaleoLoneWolf

I hit send and then reopened the email from home and stared at the picture of Molly. I swear, my baby sister's arms looked like rows of squishy marshmallows. Her legs were just a blur in the picture, so I knew she was kicking them back and forth the way she does when she gets excited. Her smile was shiny with drool. Babies are a mess. But somehow Molly pulled it off, looking adorable anyway. I could see my dad's arm stretched out behind her, ready to catch her when she flopped backward.

"Is that your sister?" Megan asked from the station on my left. I nodded and watched Megan's face as she looked at the picture. *Three, two, one . . .*

Right on cue, Megan said, "Is she—does she have—"

"Down syndrome?" I finished for her. "Yeah."

Megan nodded.

Countdown to when she starts naming all the people she knows with Down syndrome in three, two, one . . .

But Megan surprised me. "She's cute. I don't have any sisters. That I know, of anyway."

"What do you mean?"

"I'm adopted." She twisted her bracelet, then held up her wrist. "Mom gave me this bracelet when she told me, not that it was a huge surprise. I mean, I'm Korean and she's blonde. But she says it's something to always re-member that she chose to spend her life being my mom."

"That's really nice," I said. Then I felt kind of dumb. I mean, here she was telling me about her adoption and all I had to say was "that's nice." I guess that's why so many people say the same stupid things when they find out about Molly's Down syndrome. They just don't know what to say. "Is it silver? Your bracelet, I mean."

Megan nodded. "Jessica said she saw something like it online from Tiffany's."

Mr. Bosserman's giant stopwatch blared. I closed the picture of Molly and shut down the computer. "Sorry again about Jer."

"No biggie. I didn't really know him or anything," Megan said. "I've moved on, anyway." Megan swirled in her seat so she was facing Ash, and her eyes got all misty again. Aha.

Chapter Eleven

The next day of Camp Paleo was dedicated to torture, although the counselors kept referring to it as "Field Day."

So far, we had endured volleyball and kickball.

Crazily enough, a lot of these campers actually seemed to be enjoying it. I have to admit, I did laugh every time I saw Jer showing off for April.

Jer kept trying to give April tips on how to kick the ball. "Thanks, Jer, but I've got this," she finally said. "I just have to stretch a little." Then she did about ten lightning-fast roundhouse kicks, stopping a couple inches from the side of his head.

"Yeah," he said. "You've got this."

I checked out during kickball. I sort of missed the ball entirely on my first time up to kick and fell on my tailbone. Hard. (Honesty alert: Maybe not quite as hard as I made it seem. But I did get out of kickball.) Jessica walked me to the most magnificent air-conditioned oasis from Field Day torture: the eMagine nurse's office. I sat with an ice pack on my bum for a half hour. Nurse Gabby didn't seem to enjoy the company. She snapped the pages of her romance novel with way more force than necessary. As soon as thirty minutes passed, she radioed Mr. Bosserman.

"Scoot on out of here," Nurse Gabby said, not looking up from the pages of her book. "Mr. Bosserman says you're just in time for dodgeball."

Awesome.

The camp had been divided in half at the dodgeball field. Jer quickly took control of the ball and nailed every player, starting with me. I wasn't even mad, not after seeing the shot Sheldon took to the head right after my leg shot. The other shooters on Jer's team always tossed him the ball. Soon it was down to two players: Jer and April. Somehow he missed her. April was getting a scary intense look on her face, the one I normally only saw during tae kwon do practice. "Come on!" she taunted. "Try and get me!"

Jer grinned and threw the ball, hard. I thought April was done for! But no! She caught it and without even a second's hesitation hurled it back at Jer, nailing him in the stomach.

For a second, I thought Operation Dorks in Love, Phase Two was doomed. No way would he want to be April's boyfriend after she beat him like that, but again I was wrong. Jer stumbled by me, bent to hold his knees as he took a few deep breaths, and said, "She is wicked cool."

I laughed. If only he knew the real April . . .

Next up was archery, and I fought down a little spark inside. This could be it!

I sort of have a theory. I suppose it's a hunch really, since theories are supported by facts and this isn't supported by anything but hope. But I believe I'm really awesome at something. Like, so awesome I'll be interviewed by reporters and maybe even get a book deal. So incredible other people will stop what they're doing just to watch me do that thing. They'll all ask, "Lucy! Lucy! What's your secret?" And I'll just smile and shrug. "Just a natural talent," I'll say. I can feel it, this awesomeness deep inside of me, waiting to be tapped.

I just don't know what that awesome thing is yet. So anytime I try something new, I think maybe this is it. Maybe this is the thing I'm awesome at doing.

So far, I can cross off tae kwon do and any of the sports we do in gym class. It's not gymnastics, since Sam once tried to teach me how to do a cartwheel and I ended up cracking a barrette against my skull. It's not kickball, obviously, or dodgeball. I'm great at walking while chewing gum but I haven't really shared that with many people. (It's a seriously underrated skill, if you ask me.)

Mr. Bosserman and the other camp counselors divided us into groups of four and showed us the basics, like how to hold the bow.

Sheldon, Amanda, and Megan were in my group. "April!" I called out. "Why don't you join us?"

Kira strutted up and linked her arm in April's. They had styled their hair the same—again! This time pigtails. "Remember you said you'd be my partner?" she asked April, and led her over to an empty space.

"This is your chance," I hissed to Jer, who bounced next to me, super excited to try out archery.

"What?" he asked, not looking up from the arrows and bows spread out in front of us. I guess he had the same awesome-inside feeling, too. But judging how he already was incredible at every sport he tried, I thought that was being a little selfish of him.

"Go!" I jerked my chin toward April. "Get in her group."

"Who? Oh, yeah!" he said and headed in April's direction. I sighed, wondering why I go to so much trouble for people who clearly do not appreciate me. Soon he was just behind her, laughing too loudly at something she said.

A little squeak behind me reminded me of Megan's new crush. Ash was headed toward April's group, too. No! I couldn't let that happen. "Ash!" I called, waving my arms wildly. "Over here! Over here!"

"But we already have four," Sheldon pointed out.

Amanda counted us all again. "Yeah."

"Don't worry about it," I said as Ash joined us. "It's not like we have an even number of people in camp."

"Yes, we do," Ash said. "There are twenty all together."

"Well, Sheldon and Amanda count as one lately. I've already started thinking of them as Shemanda."

Our counselor—the one with whom Jessica had been spending all week flirting with—didn't agree. "You!" he snapped. "Head over to Mr. Bosserman's group."

Any guesses which one of us he pointed to? Mr. Bosserman sighed as I approached. Then he went down to the target and scooted it down a few feet away from the other campers, shaking his head and muttering about "fool-headed kids" the whole time.

Mr. Bosserman demonstrated how to use the bow and then we all lined up in long rows, facing the haystacks with targets pinned on the front. Mr. Bosserman counted down, then *swoosh*! Our arrows were set free! I kept my eyes squeezed shut, wanting them to burst open to a display of awesomeness.

"Wow!" Someone in my group said.

"Way to go!" Someone else cheered.

I opened my eyes, certain the arrow had flown right into the red center circle. But nope, no arrow. Where did it go? Maybe it flew so hard it went right through the haystack! And then I saw it, hanging limply from the side of the haystack, not even near the widest circle on the target. I sighed and slumped forward to collect it when Mr. Bosserman gave the okay.

"What's with cheering for me when I totally suck at this?" I snapped at the kid behind me.

His face twisted. "What are you talking about?"

"Yeah." The girl waiting behind him laughed. "We weren't cheering for *you*. We were cheering for April."

Sure enough, April stood two stations down from me with the bow in place. She shot arrow after arrow straight into the bulls-eye. *Swoosh, swoosh, swoosh*!

How did she get to be awesome at tae kwon do *and* archery! This was so not fair!

Kira bumped April's shoulder as she got another arrow from the pile beside her. Facing me, Kira said, loud enough for the whole camp to hear, "Check out jealousy over there!" And everyone turned toward me. April gave a little half wave, not in a mean way, either. Just a wave.

"Good job, April!" I called, but it sounded fake, even to me.

Come on, Lucy! I told myself. *We can do this. We can show them!* I got another arrow and loaded it, sure that this time the awesome would shine through and Kira would have to shut her stupid mouth. I closed my eyes and let it fly. I didn't even look again, just loaded another like April.

"Hey!" a kid at the station beside me snapped. "Stick to your own target!"

"What?" I turned toward him, arrow still in the bow.

He screamed and hit the ground with a thud, just like everyone behind him. "Crazy freak!" he yelled.

I thrust the bow at Mr. Bosserman. "I'm done with this."

"You didn't really give it much of a shot," he pointed out. "I think it takes more than two tries for someone to learn this, onest."

"Not everyone," I said, watching April nail another arrow to the haystack.

Chapter Twelve

The next morning, I woke up with half my body out of the sleeping bag and still covered in sweat. No breeze, just a blanket of damp, hot air suffocating me. And the sun wasn't even up yet.

"Wake up, sleepyheads!" Jessica chirped. "It's our day to make breakfast!"

A few minutes later, April and I stood behind the grill with huge spatulas, pushing the "eggs" Amanda poured onto the surface from a jug.

Megan took forever in the bathroom. When she finally joined us, I saw tear tracks down her cheeks.

"What's wrong?" I asked.

Megan held up her wrist. "My bracelet! It's gone." She hiccupped. "I put it in my bathroom bag before Field Day yesterday so it wouldn't get knocked around or snagged during the games. I went to put it back on after my shower. But it's not in my bag! I looked everywhere."

"Maybe it's off somewhere with my *designer* makeup bag," Kira said from her perch on a nearby picnic table.

"Anything else missing?" April asked.

Megan shook her head.

Jessica put her arm around Megan and squeezed. In her relentlessly cheery way, she said, "Maybe it fell out of the bag on the way to the bathroom. I bet it'll turn up."

"You said the same thing about my makeup bag. It hasn't yet," Kira pointed out. Megan hiccupped again.

Jessica told Megan that getting busy would help her forget about the bracelet, so she stationed her behind an enormous vat of hot cocoa. Megan stirred it with a huge spoon. I guess we had run out of watery OJ.

"Could you maybe help out?" I asked Kira.

She yawned and stretched her arms. Super slowly, she started stacking napkins and plates. "Happy?" she asked, then skipped off to the farthest picnic table.

"How can you put up with her?" I asked April, shoving a spatula full of eggs across the grill. A glob of powder broke apart. They turned kind of greenish for a second while they cooked.

April shrugged. "She's not all bad. She can be kind of funny."

"She's a Becky." I shuddered, thinking of my former best friend, the one who would only be nice to me in secret. And even then, she was horrible.

"No, she isn't." April shoved the eggs back toward me. "Everything Becky did was to make other people like her. Kira doesn't care who likes her."

"What's with you lately?" I snapped, pushing the eggs back. "It's like I don't even know you."

April glared at the eggs and didn't answer, so I kept talking. "Do you even care about us anymore? I mean, you let her talk about me. You spend more time with Ash than you do with us. You were too busy showing off during Field Day to even notice I had gotten hurt."

April sighed and slammed down her spatula, splattering me with egg juice. "All you do is whine. Everything is Lucy, Lucy, Lucy!" She picked up the spatula and jabbed me with it, her eyes wild. "When was the last time you did anything for *me*? When are you—any of you!—there for *me*?"

"Listen, chicas, how about we all meditate a bit before we continue here?" Amanda said, pouring another jug of eggs onto the grill. She hummed *kumbaya*.

"What are you talking about?" I jabbed April back with my spatula, sending a few egg globs onto the ground.

April threw down her spatula, which landed with a thud in the dirt. "I'm talking about *me*. I want something of *mine*. Not to be just a backup member of your stupid little pack." She stomped off.

"Stupid?" I screamed at her back. "It wasn't so stupid when we were the only friends you had!"

April turned and rushed me, and I remembered for a knee-knocking moment that she is a totally kick-butt martial artist. She got so close I could see the sweat glistening on her forehead. "You are just as bad as Kira. Maybe worse! At least Kira doesn't try to control her friends. If I start talking differently or wearing my hair differently, she doesn't care."

"Yeah, because you talk like *her*. You wear your hair like *her*." I held up my spatula like a shield. Behind me, I heard Megan squeak-cry when I stepped back onto her toe.

"I told you she was just jealous of you." Kira stood behind April, her hip leaning against the picnic table like she was bored out of her mind. Then she turned and walked off.

April stared at me a second before following Kira.

"Maybe you don't know this," Megan said, extra quietly behind me, "since you normally sleep in to the last minute every morning. But April's up first. She does her hair first. Kira is trying to be like April, not the other way around."

"That's ridiculous." I crossed my arms.

You know what stinks more than having a huge fight with one of your best friends in front of your nemesis? Nothing.

Except maybe one thing.

After April left with Kira, I stood there stunned for about five minutes. That's about how long it takes for eggs to turn into crusty, black bits that make Scott, this boy in Sheldon's A-frame who put on swim trunks the first day and hasn't changed since, smell like flowers.

"Oh no! The 'eggs' are burning!" I yelled.

"Why do you make little air quotes when you say eggs?" Amanda asks. "It makes me angry."

"Because they aren't real eggs. They're a powdery and green and gross egg-like substance."

"They're eggs. No air quotes," Amanda snapped.

"No. The air quotes indicate that while some people, ahem, Mr. Bosserman, say they're eggs, they're not really. They're 'eggs.'"

"But they're made from eggs. So they're eggs." Amanda clenched her fists.

"Listen, eggs are disgusting enough. I mean, we're eating something squeezed out of a chicken's butt. Why do we have to eat 'eggs' that are even grosser?"

"*Kumbaya. Kumbaya.*" Amanda took a deep breath. "When you think about it, everything is disgusting. A disgusting miracle."

"Huh. You're really getting spiritual."

"Guys! The eggs are burning!" Megan pointed to clouds of blackish smoke puffing up from the crustified egg mixture. She waved her arms over the small flames but ended up sending a stack of paper napkins over the grill. They smoldered and quickly burst into red flames, too.

"We have to do something!" I screamed. "Where is Jessica?"

I spotted her red hair across the campsite, talking with the counselor who bunked in Sheldon's A-frame—she was totally ignoring us.

Amanda took some deep breaths. "We need to—*puff*—calm—*puff*—down!"

"Aaahh!" I whapped on the side of Megan's huge vat of hot cocoa, spilling it over the grill and dousing the flames.

We all sighed softly as the horrendous stench was squelched by the comforting aroma of chocolate.

"That was a close one," Megan murmured.

I put my fist up for a bump all around, but no one took me up on it. "We are in huge trouble," Amanda murmured.

I lowered my fist.

Jessica stomped across the lawn, screaming, "What have you done?" Campers trickled out of their A-frames and toward the picnic tables. They covered their noses with their hands or the tops of their T-shirts.

Mr. Bosserman surged forward, waving his arms to get through the groaning crowd like he was swatting away gnats. When he got to the front, I could see why his son put him in charge of a caveman camp. He stomped around, grunting, gesturing toward the still-smoking-cocoa-soaked grill, the egg juice all over the floor, the spatula in the dirt. Jessica scooted toward the front, saw Mr. Bosserman's scary purple face, and stepped back.

"What happened here?" he bellowed.

Amanda shrugged. "Well, first Lucy picked a fight with April. Then she got into a fight with me." She leaned into Mr. Bosserman and lowered her voice. "Between you and me, I think she has some anger issues."

"Fool-headed kids! Now what are we supposed to do?"

"Um." I put down my spatula. "Is there a diner nearby?"

Mr. Bosserman stomped to the back of the campsite with Jessica while the rest of the campers sat down at picnic tables. Mr. Bosserman and Jessica were far enough away that I couldn't hear what they said, only that he was yelling. A lot. He gestured toward all of us and Jessica walked back without any of her usual perkiness while he yelled some more into a phone.

Jessica stormed toward me with scary straight robot arms and stiff legs. Her usual smile was totally wiped off her face. Instead, her lips were pressed in a white line. "You!" She pointed at me. "Do you have any idea what you've done?"

I sucked on my lip, not sure how to respond.

"She burned breakfast?" Amanda offered.

"And got me fired! I can't go losing a kid one day and having her destroy the entire campsite's meal the next. Ugh! This was supposed to count toward my community service college credit!" Jessica shuddered. "I hate kids! Hate them!" She kicked the downed spatula and stomped off to our A-frame.

Amanda gave a low whistle a second later when we heard a massive ripping sound. "There goes the kitten poster."

Soon we heard a rumbling sound as a golf cart rolled down the dirt path toward our site. It parked in front of us and Grandma climbed out. "What did you do now, Toots?" she asked me.

"Darn kid wrecked breakfast, that's what." Mr. Bosserman's face was slowly going back to normal color, but still sort of pinkish.

"It was an accident," I mumbled. "April and I had a fight." I peeked up at Grandma and saw that she was studying my face. Suddenly my knees got shaky again. My chin shook a little. If all these people weren't here, staring at me, I'd rush forward and bury my face in Grandma's mushy waist. I really wanted my mom, but Grandma would do, too.

"Buck up." Grandma nodded at me. "It's all right."

"It's *what*?" Mr. Bosserman snapped.

Grandma ignored him, getting out a box filled with single-serve cereals from the backseat. It was like one of those scenes in Robin Hood movies where he gives loaves of bread to peasants. Everyone rushed forward, hands out, grabbing at little boxes of corn flakes and cocoa rice. Grandma opened another box and began throwing apples and clementines to the cluster of starving campers.

Over the cheers for Grandma, Mr. Bosserman continued yelling, "That girl needs a tighter rope! She's out of control, thinking she can just run off when she feels like it. Shoot arrows with her eyes shut. Wreck meals. I don't know if we can get that grill running again!"

Grandma whipped around to him, thrusting the box of fruit into his chest. Her eyes narrowed behind her smudgy glasses and her lips pursed. "Don't you go blaming Lucy. She's a kid. Where were you? Where was the supervision?"

"I'm dealing with the counselor who should've been there," Mr. Bosserman grumped. "Don't get in a fret."

"Did you just tell me not to 'get in a fret'?" Grandma pushed forward so her forehead was an inch from Mr. Bosserman's forehead. Some of his frizzy white hair had to be tickling her cheek.

Mr. Bosserman stepped back. "Sorry."

Grandma smiled and then lowered herself into the golf cart. She smoothed her fingers across her apron. "We still on for tonight?" she asked as she turned the key in the ignition.

"Nine o'clock, right?" Mr. Bosserman asked. "I made shoo fly pie."

She nodded, making her chin wobble. Then Grandma pointed at me. "Clean up this mess, Luc."

I knew she wasn't just talking about the grill.

After scrubbing the grill for about a half hour, Mr. Bosserman told me to get lost. Actually he said, "Quit your brutzing and moaning and let it rest."

I think I got the translation right and even tried speaking a little Mr. Bosserman. "I got in a fret with April. Have you seen her?"

"Maybe let it go awhile," he said. "Let her calm down."

"Nah, I'll be rutching until I talk to her."

"Go check the A-frame. Think I saw her there."

"Thanks, Mr. Bosserman. And sorry about the grill."

I found my former friend on a grassy area behind our A-frame. She whipped through tae kwon do forms with way more force than necessary.

If you don't know about tae kwon do, here's a quick lesson. First: if your instructor is an old purple walnut lady named Miss Betsy, you're probably going to hate your first class. Second: if you make it to the second class, you're going to find out that it's a real sport, not a throw-a-punch-there-add-a-kick-here sort of thing. Forms are a way to sort of showcase what you know. The first time I showed Mom and Dad a form, they said it looked like a dance. In a lot of ways, I guess it is. But even though we do the same steps, April's dance is much more complex than mine. She pours everything into her forms, where I just try to not mess up the steps.

It reminded me suddenly of Shemanda doing yoga on the lakeshore the day before. Maybe this was April's meditation. If it was, then she was seriously looking for some Zen. And I knew I was the one who made her so mad.

Just as I was about to say her name, someone else beat me to it. "April! That's awesome!" I hadn't seen Kira sitting at the base of a tree trunk. "I'm going to take tae kwon do when camp's over."

April grinned, wiping her forehead with the hem of her T-shirt. "Yeah, it's hard, but it's a lot of fun."

Her easy smile was a windshield wiper, pushing aside all my guilt. Anger pelted me in its place. Here I thought April was working off steam after our fight when she was really just showing off!

"Is there anything you're not good at?" Kira asked.

April's face flushed and she laughed. "Tons of things!"

"Name three."

"Um . . ."

"That's what I thought!" Kira said. "You can't even think of three faults."

"I could tell you three things." I stepped off the A-frame toward them, letting all my meanness flare through me, starting at my toes and erupting through my mouth. I held up one finger. "She doesn't stand up for her friends." A second finger. "She's always trying to be someone she's not." A third finger. "She still picks her nose at night. She used to all of the time, until *I* convinced her it was gross."

My hands flew to my mouth, trying to cram the words back inside. But it was too late. April's eyes filled with tears. I thought she'd yell at me, but what she did was even worse. She whispered, "I hate you."

I stood there shaking, wanting to tell her I hated her, too. But I couldn't.

"Come on," said Kira, putting an arm around April and turning her away from me. "She's not worth it."

Chapter Thirteen

Even Shemanda was mad at me.

When I walked up to them later (after spending about an hour or so crying into my mattress), they turned their backs to me. "We heard what you said to April," Sheldon said over his shoulder.

"And it's terrible," Amanda finished.

"She's happy here. She's popular," Sheldon spit out.

"Why can't you be happy for her?" Amanda added.

Sheldon and Amanda looked at each other and shook their heads. "Wait a second, where's the trilobite?" Sheldon asked.

Amanda's hand flew to her neck. "The string! It was fraying a little, so I took it off while we were making breakfast!"

They rushed to the picnic tables to look for the fossil. Mr. Bosserman called out that we had an hour of free time before our next adventure: canoe riding on the lake. We were supposed to spend the time with our friends. I stomped into the woods—alone.

I sat down on a log and pulled out a granola bar I'd stashed in my pocket. A few seconds later, leaves rustled behind me. I guess someone finally noticed I was missing. I turned to see, but no one was there. Huh? I nibbled on the bar. More rustling.

This time when I turned around, a fat squirrel stared at me. He sat on his back legs a few feet away. I held out a piece of granola and the squirrel slowly stepped forward on its two back legs. Suddenly I remembered Sam telling me about his cousin, who got bit by an albino squirrel at a nature center. He said its rodent teeth of pain latched onto her finger and wouldn't let go until she twirled around three times.

Probably the only thing worse than being friendless at camp is being friendless at camp with a squirrel stuck to your finger. I broke off a piece of granola and threw it, hitting Mr. Chubs in the head. I thought he'd run off, but he didn't. He turned the piece around in his paws and nibbled alongside me. This is what my life had come to, getting sympathy from a squirrel.

Mr. Chubs stuck around until Sheldon started yelling. Even though he was back at the picnic area, Sheldon shouted loud enough for me to hear and Mr. Chubs to freak out and run. "It's three hundred fifty million years old!" Sheldon screamed. "It's not like it just got up and scurried off on its own!"

"I put it right here!" Amanda yelled back. "Right here!"

"I thought it meant something to you!"

"It does!"

I strained to hear Sheldon's quiet response. "It's okay. We'll find it. Don't worry."

Oh man. It was like listening to one of those made-for-TV movies that make Mom all weepy on Sunday afternoons. Only this one involved creepy shrimpy-looking fossils.

I probably would've fallen asleep there in the woods, but Mr. Bosserman called us all to get ready for canoeing. Sheldon and Amanda held hands as they walked toward the other campers.

Later that horrible day, during screen time, I pulled up the Camp Paleo blogger site to see if SSCPB had answered my question. She did.

Dear LoneWolf:

No. It's never okay. Ever. No wonder you're alone.

SSCPB

Well, that was direct.

I shifted my gaze to the back table where April sat with Kira. Jer was there, too, peppering April with baseball facts he'd read online. She put on earbuds.

I spent the rest of the screen time hour ignoring the ping of Sam's Skype requests and the feeling that every other camper's eyes were boring into the back of my head.

They're not staring at you, I told myself. *They've all got much better things to do than worry about you.* Even my inner voice sounded disappointed in me.

I ended up on the Able Wolf Sanctuary website. Under the "Meet the Pack" subhead, I found the profile for Sascha and Ralph. It read:

"For the longest time, Sascha was so determined to be the Alpha wolf that she wouldn't connect with anyone else, even when they weren't trying to take the top spot from her. This determination to be number one ended up keeping her alone. It wasn't until we took a chance that she'd connect with Ralph—another wolf everyone had given up on—that she finally made a connection. We won't say everything's been easy since that day. Sascha has really given us a run for the money, and we mean that figuratively and literally. She's tried to run away about a half-dozen times." I could see sanctuary owner, Adam Able's, mustache twitching as he typed the lame joke.

I kept reading. "Ralph has gotten stronger, too, and has stood up to Sascha a few times. Thanks to his generally even temperament, we've even been able to introduce a couple other wolves who might become permanent members of Pack Sascha.

"While it's natural for a wolf to establish a hierarchy, or order of importance, among a pack, we hope that Sascha's need to be alpha doesn't ultimately cost her the best and only companions she's made."

I clicked "Accept" during Sam's next Skype request, but it was too late. Screen time was over. I only saw a flash of his face.

We had dinner at the eMagine mess hall that night since the grill was still reeking of hot-cocoa eggs. I thought I'd get a few "thank yous" for this minor miracle, but nope. Once again, I was a solo eater in the cafeteria. Grandma, at least, gave me an extra scoop of refried beans.

I lingered toward the end of the line back to the A-frame. I had this wild hope that everyone else would be asleep by the time I arrived and I wouldn't have to deal with April and Kira hating me. But no such luck.

Kira sat on the stoop, a small, smug smile on her face. "You really did it this time."

I ignored her and walked into the A-frame. Every single person stopped midsentence. The room was a disaster, worse than when Kira had freaked out over her missing designer makeup bag. Clothes were scattered all over the room, and it looked like someone took a bathroom bag and dumped all of the shampoo, conditioner, and soap bottles, along with toothbrush and toothpaste, onto the floor. Wait a sec. Not just any bathroom bag. *My* bathroom bag. And all the clothes? They were mine, too.

"What is going on?" I yelled.

Kira sauntered back into the A-frame, leaning against the side and crossing her arms. "Seems like something else has gone missing. April's laptop."

"What? April, you can't think I would—"

"A little suspicious, don't you think?" Kira continued. "Every single one of us has something expensive stolen from our A-frame. Everyone, that is, but you."

"That's because I don't have anything expensive to steal!" I snapped. Both Mom and Dad worked hard but there wasn't a lot of extra cash for expensive toys.

Jessica stood, her hands up. I wasn't surprised that she was still hanging around. Even though Mr. Bosserman said she was fired, I didn't think he actually was going to go through with it. Besides, he still had to find a replacement counselor. I think she thought if she did a good job keeping us quiet, he might change his mind. "Now, now, camper wampers! No one said anything about stealing. That's a biggie word there!"

I looked to Amanda for help, but she sat cross-legged on her bunk, hands resting on her knees and chanting. From the sound of her jaws grinding, I don't think the meditation was helping.

April crossed her arms and turned away from me.

"April, you know me!" I whispered. "You know I would never steal anything."

"I thought I knew you," she said. "But now I'm not so sure."

"Come on now, campers." Jessica held up her hands in a stopping motion.

"What do you care?" Kira turned on Jessica. "I heard what Mr. Bosserman told you after our breakfast fiasco. You're out of here the second your mom comes to pick you up."

Jessica's face flamed for a moment and her fists clenched. I think if there had been another kitten poster nearby, it would've been shredded. Then she took a deep breath and in her usual chipper voice said, "Let's get cleaned up and ready for bed. I'm sure everything will turn up soon."

"You're really fired?" I asked. "I thought Mr. Bosserman was just brutzing. I didn't think he'd actually . . ."

"Yes, she's fired," Kira said. "Thanks to you."

Jessica crossed her arms and glared at me. I opened my mouth to say sorry, but she turned away.

"But what if our stuff doesn't turn up?" Megan asked, not looking at me. "Someone has been stealing our stuff. We should call the cops."

"The cops?" Jessica's eyes widened. "Whoa, now! I'm in enough trouble. Mr. Bosserman would probably call my college and get me in trouble there, too, if cops get involved in our campsite when I'm in charge. Please, guys. Please, let's just do a thorough search."

I slumped over to my bunk, putting my things one by one back into my bag. April and Amanda piled things onto my bed while Kira, Jessica, and Megan searched the rest of the A-frame.

"Hey! Look at this!" Jessica called suddenly from the A-frame entrance. She held up a bracelet.

"Is that yours?" April asked Megan.

Megan twisted the bracelet so it was inside out and read the inscription. "To Megan, the baby of my heart. Love, Mom." Her face shined. "Yes! It's mine. Thank you, Jessica!" She threw her arms around the counselor.

"See!" I shouted. "I didn't take anything!"

Everyone ignored me.

Jessica patted her back. "I told you it probably just slipped out of your bathroom bag! See, I'm sure every-thing else will turn up, too."

"What about my bag?"

"And my laptop?"

"And my trilobite?"

Kira crossed her arms and glared at me. "You're not off the hook yet."

Jessica waved her hands. "Let's just get to bed. If Mr. Bosserman sees we're all still up . . ." Her usual perky face was twisted with worry. "I'd be in real trouble."

"Okay," April agreed. "Maybe someone found my laptop and returned it to the computer lab."

"I'm sure of it!" Jessica clapped. She flipped off the overhead light and everyone settled into their bunks. I waited until I heard steady breathing from all around except above me.

"April?" I whispered.

"Go to bed, Lucy." April's voice was frosty. "I don't want to talk to you now. Maybe not ever."

Have you ever felt like things have gotten so bad, they couldn't possibly get any worse?

Listen to me: they can always get worse.

I lay awake most of the night, thinking about how and why so many things had gone wrong. I made a mental list of the problems.

Problem one: April changed. From the time we got to Camp Paleo, she stopped being the April I thought I knew. From the way she wears her hair to how she speaks, she's different. The April I know—the April in my pack—is a dork. She says everything in bursts. She doesn't worry about her hair. She's not some athletic superstar.

And then this annoying voice inside started talking to me, saying maybe that was just the April I thought I knew. Maybe Pack April talked in bursts because no one gave her a chance to stretch out her thoughts. Maybe Pack April was only a dork because everyone expected her to be one. It's like SSCPB said in her post: *Camp should be a time for you to live the way you want to live, nobody breathing down your neck about how to act or who to be.* Maybe that's what April had been doing all along, and I was too stubborn to notice. Maybe Camp April was the real April. And the real April hated me.

Problem two: I had lied to Jer about April liking him and to Megan about Ash liking her. If April hated me now, that was nothing compared to how she'd feel if she found out about the lie. I crossed my fingers she'd never find out. And Megan? She'd be crushed. Little voice said this problem needed to be figured out pronto.

Problem three: Shemanda was mad at me. The little voice whispered that Sam would be, too, when he found out about my fight with April. I told the voice that Sam wasn't even here so it should just shut up about Sam.

Problem four: the thefts. Who was stealing all of our stuff? This time the little voice was testy and pointed out that none of my stuff was worthy of stealing. I again told it to shut up.

Problem five: Jessica was getting fired because of me. Little voice hissed that this should make me feel guiltier than it did.

Problem six: a mosquito bit my butt in the bathroom and it was super uncomfortable. The little voice told me to be grateful I wasn't the girl in the neighboring A-frame who couldn't make it to the bathroom during our hike and squatted in poison ivy.

Chapter Fourteen

When the sun came up, I made a decision.

Not a decision to be happy, because I know that never works when your life is crumbling to pieces. A decision to put the pieces back together. Then maybe I could be happy.

First up, swing by Nurse Gabby's for Calamine Lotion for my butt bite. Little voice is telling me that was TMI, but I just didn't want you to worry.

Second: Shemanda.

I found them by the picnic tables, hashing out a plan for where to find another fossil. Both of them turned toward me with crossed arms. Maybe this wouldn't be as easy as I hoped.

"Listen." I took a deep breath and let out the little speech I had prepared. "I'm sorry about the mess I made with April, and I'm sorry that your trilobite is missing. I hope you know that I never, ever would steal from you or anyone."

They looked at one another. Amanda nodded.

"Yeah," Sheldon said. "We know. You do a lot of stupid things, but you don't steal."

"But we're not getting involved in this April thing," Amanda finished.

"Understood. I'm going to fix things. I swear!" I bounced on my heels a second. "Thanks, Shemanda!" I threw my arms around them.

"You're welcome," they said together. As I walked away, I heard Sheldon whisper, "Did she just call us Shemanda?"

Here's the plan for solving the Jer problem. Brace yourself—it's a shocker.

I'm going to tell him the truth.

I'm just going to go up to him, tell him I'd lied and that April wasn't just playing hard to get. I didn't know if she liked him in that way. I would tell him I'm sorry and that it was wrong of me.

Chances are, he wouldn't forgive me. But I kind of deserved that. And, with any luck, I'd never see him again after the end of this week.

I had to tell him and quick. "April! April!" I heard him call from a picnic table on the other side of the camp. "Check it out!" He was juggling a grapefruit, an apple, and an orange. April nodded in his direction and went back to talking with Kira and a bunch of other girls from a different A-frame. How did she know everyone? Seriously, every Camp Paleo camper seemed to know April. A lot of them were clustered around her now.

"April! April!" Jer called again. Now he was juggling while jumping from foot to foot.

I had to put this kid out of his misery. The closer I got to Jer, the more April turned away. I guess Jer didn't realize it was because she hates me and not because his juggling/jumping show wasn't impressive enough, because he snagged a second grapefruit off the picnic table and added it to the mix. He started kicking it around like one of his hacky sacks while still juggling the other grapefruit, apple, and orange.

"April! April!"

April turned around to appease Jer just as I moved right behind him. She locked eyes with me, sighed super deeply, and turned back around.

Jer called for a kid to toss him another piece of fruit, which he added to the juggling routine.

"Jer," I said. "I need to talk to you."

"Back up, Lucy. I'm not exactly sure how to stop this." Grapefruit, orange, grapefruit, apple, and plum swirled between us. I moved so I was between him and April, forcing him to see me.

"You're in my way," Jer sighed. "I can't see April!"

"This is *about* April," I hissed back at him, watching the blur of fruit.

Jer missed the apple and it landed on the ground between us. "What about her?"

"She doesn't really like you. I made it up."

"Haha. Very funny. Of course she likes me." Grapefruit, orange, grapefruit, plum.

"No, really." I focused on his face, not the flying fruit. "I lied. She's not playing hard to get. She's not into you. I'm sorry."

Jer stared at me with huge, green eyes. His hands fell to his sides.

"You what?" April yelled, standing right behind me.

Crap sandwich.

Grapefruit, orange, and plum hit the ground. I quickstepped back before the second grapefruit fell. "Look out!" I shouted.

The squishy slam of grapefruit hitting April will haunt my dreams. After impact, April didn't cry or even make a sound. She just sort of folded over onto herself. I caught her before she hit the ground. "April!" I screamed. Her eyes fluttered a little and then her arms flung out.

"She's disoriented!" I screamed to the gathering crowd. "She doesn't know what she's doing!"

Suddenly, April's eyes popped open and she pushed me with two hands, sending me onto my butt. "I am trying to get away from *you!*" she screamed. "Get away from me!"

"Back again?" Nurse Gabby opened her door to my tear-stained face.

"Not her!" Jer elbowed me aside. "April!" He and Ash each had an arm around April. "She took a grapefruit to the temple." April held the grapefruit up as evidence.

"Oh, dear," Nurse Gabby said. "Did she lose consciousness?"

"Only for a second," I said. "It was just a grapefruit."

Nurse Gabby nodded. "You'd be surprised. I once had a patient who got a concussion from a yoyo."

"Concussion!" April gasped.

Nurse Gabby prodded the bruise on April's temple. "Not a lot of swelling."

"That's good, right?" I asked.

Nurse Gabby frowned. "It could mean the swelling has gone inward."

"Why are you still here?" April snapped at me, but her words ran into each other. Her eyes drifted shut and then snapped back open.

"Tired?" Nurse Gabby asked.

April nodded and Nurse Gabby eased her head onto the pillow at the top of the cot.

"I'm so sorry, April!" I yelled as Nurse Gabby shooed us out. April didn't move, just laid there like Snow White, holding a grapefruit instead of a poisoned apple.

Ash and Jer turned on me as the door snapped shut.

"You know," Ash said, "I defended you when my sister said you were mean and selfish. April said you were her friend, so I figured Kira was wrong. But she wasn't, was she?"

Jer stared at me with wide, green eyes. "Why would you lie to me like that?"

I opened my mouth to answer, but nothing came out. Because there was no way I could justify what I did. I had become a Becky, pushing someone to do something just because it was what I wanted. No. I was worse than Becky.

Becky only hurt me. I had hurt lots of people.

Like it was on cue, Megan ran up the path to Nurse Gabby's office. "I heard," she huffed, putting her hands on her knees to breathe. She must've run the whole way from the picnic areas.

"Is April okay?"

"She has a concussion," Jer said. "Thanks to Lucy." He turned to face Megan. "If she hadn't lied to me about April liking me I wouldn't have even juggled. April likes Ash, not me."

"She doesn't like me!" Ash gasped. "We are seriously just friends. I don't like any girls here."

"But you said Ash likes me!" Megan whipped toward me.

Ash's mouth dropped open. "I don't like you." At Megan's squeak, he put his hand out. "I mean, I don't like you that way. I'm not into . . . I'm not ready . . ." Ash's fists clenched and he stomped his foot. "Thanks a lot, Lucy," he whispered and then stomped off.

"I can't believe you," Megan hissed and walked away.

"Wait up," Jer called as he ran toward her.

I sank back down on Nurse Gabby's stoop.

Nurse Gabby came to the stoop with her cell phone in hand about a half hour later. "Is she going to be all right?" I asked.

"She should be," the nurse said. "Not a lot of statistics on concussion by grapefruit. I need to call her parents."

"Does she have to go home?" I asked.

"Nah, but she'll need to take it easy. No more swimming, archery, or any of the other Camp Paleo stuff. It's all bad for the recently concussed."

"Recently concussed?" I raised an eyebrow at Nurse Gabby, wondering if she had made up a word.

Her eyes scanned me on the stoop. "Why don't you head back? It's got to be close to dinnertime."

"I'll stay here, if that's okay," I said.

Nurse Gabby looked up from her phone. "You must be a good friend to her."

I shook my head. "No, I'm not."

❖ ❖ ❖

Grandma came to bring April dinner an hour later. She shook my shoulder and woke me from where I'd fallen asleep on the stoop.

"Want me to tell her hi from you?" Grandma asked.

I shook my head again.

Grandma handed me a cookie, but I didn't take it.

"Hang in there, Toots," she said, and put a ham sandwich next to me on her way back to the cafeteria.

Shemanda stopped by the nurse's office on their way to screen time and told me that a bunch of things—a wallet, an iPhone, and an expensive pair of sneakers—were stolen from Sheldon's A-frame while the campers had been swimming. "Nothing of mine was taken," Sheldon said. "I guess the thief doesn't appreciate the value of geological rock picks."

"Don't feel bad," I said. "The thief didn't take anything from me, either."

Whoever it was, the thief only targeted expensive items.

"Why don't you come with us?" Amanda asked as they left the office. "The nurse told us April has to stay for another hour, then she'll get to go back to the A-frame."

I started to say no but changed my mind. I wasn't sure I was ready to see April once she left the office. Plus, I could try to find her laptop in the meantime.

I read the SSCPB post from yesterday.

Dear Campers:

We are winding down here at Camp Paleo. Only a few more days of camp! Think about what you've learned these past two weeks. For me, that goes way beyond dodging a ball or shooting an arrow. I've learned that I can start fresh, be anyone I want to be. The only trouble is, some people don't want you to change. They might like you just the way you were. Or maybe they like how the old you makes them feel.

Don't let that hold you back, fearless camper! Be yourself anyway.

I'll reveal a little more about myself: I got this gig as your SSCPB by writing an essay. TechSquare owner Alan Bridgeway himself wrote me back, letting me know I was named your blogger. He said he liked that I was going to take these two weeks to really figure out what I liked about me and what I didn't. He told me he started Camp Paleo just for this reason, based on how he and his dad traveled and camped when he was a kid. When it was just the two of them, roughing it, he said he saw possibilities everywhere. Sometimes, he said, he didn't like what he saw. He even would go out of his way to not go camping with his dad because it made him face some hard truths about who he was and what he wanted. He said he'd be checking in on me at the end of these two weeks to find out what I've learned.

What would you tell Mr. Bridgeway, fellow campers?

Let me know,

Your Friendly But Different SSCPB

I sucked on my bottom lip for a long time, thinking about those words. I hoped Mr. Bosserman would get a chance to read this post and understand that his son wasn't avoiding *him* when he didn't want to travel every summer. Sometimes he was avoiding himself.

Was I doing that? Was I meddling into so many people's lives because I didn't want to look at my own life? What was I scared of, really?

Little voice kept whispering Sam's name to me. I told it to simmer down. I had to fix all these messes I'd made before I saw Sam next. He'd be so mad at me. Even worse, he'd be disappointed.

I swallowed some guilt and Skype-called Sam, but he didn't answer. It was like he had given up on me, too.

I checked the lost-and-found section of the computer lab, but can't say I was surprised that April's laptop wasn't there. Someone at Camp Paleo had sticky fingers. But who?

First Kira's designer makeup bag, snagged at the beginning of camp. I wasn't ready to cross Kira off the list of potential culprits. I'd seen way too many crime shows for that. It's classic to make yourself appear like a victim to throw off the heat.

The next theft was more than a week later, when Megan's bracelet went missing. Of course, this could've been an accident, not a theft, since Jessica found it in the A-frame. But that same day, Amanda's trilobite disappeared.

The next night, April's laptop.

And today, someone snagged three things from the boys.

Whoever it was, she was stepping up her game. It smacked to me of being desperate. Maybe it was just that camp was ending in three days. Or maybe it was something else.

I kept coming back to one person.

Chapter Fifteen

We left screen time and made our way to eMagine's mess hall for dinner. The grill still smelled like eggs and charred chocolate when ignited, so we'd be having dinner in the mess hall for the remaining camp days.

And I meant to go there. I really did. During my hours of solitude, I'd promised myself to stop the meddling, sneaking, lying ways that had gotten me into this no-friends-pile-of-problems-and-April-concussed mess. But my feet didn't turn toward the mess hall. They kept right on going toward the Camp Paleo site.

As I got closer to my A-frame, my heart hammered and my lungs demanded way more air than usual. If my hunch was right and I could prove it, April might be so happy to have her laptop back she'd forgive me for lying to Jer and telling Kira about her boogie-picking past. I stopped outside of the A-frame and listened hard.

There was definitely someone rustling around in there!

Gathering all of my courage, I ninja-jumped into the A-frame, yelling "Kee-yah!" and striking a fighting stance that would make Miss Betsy proud.

Only the person I suspected wasn't there.

Instead, I faced April.

"What are you doing here?" she gasped. She, too, was in fighting stance. Both of us awkwardly lowered our arms.

"I'm trying to catch the thief."

"Me, too. I came here instead of heading to the mess hall when Nurse Gabby told me I could leave." April threw her arm around the A-frame. I followed the gesture, taking in the overturned beds. "I think I know who did it."

I tried not to smile too wide at April's words. She was talking to me! Inside, I squealed like Megan, but outside I worked on keeping my lips level. "Me, too."

April righted Megan's mattress and smoothed Kira's sleeping bag so it looked like it had that morning. "Let's say who we think it is at the same time. Three, two, one—"

We said the same name.

Jessica.

"It just makes the most sense," I said. "Everything was taken when we were out of the A-frame but still together in other parts of the camp."

"Like during screen time!" April added. "And she only took things that could be resold. Remember how she asked Kira how much her bag was worth? And she noted that Megan's bracelet is pure silver? Everything she took was expensive."

I hadn't thought of that, but it made the trilobite and sneaker snatching make more sense. "We've got to find her stash so we can prove it."

"Yeah, and her mom comes to pick her up in the morning. If we don't find it now, we might not ever!"

I looked around the mess in the A-frame. "Did you do this?"

April's face flushed a little. "I was trying to find the stolen stuff and sort of got carried away."

"I'll start putting things back where they belong. When I can't find something at home, Mom always makes me clean up. I always end up finding it."

"Cool," April said. "I'll check the perimeter."

I grinned, glad to be on the same side again. "April, I'm—"

"Save it, Lucy," April snapped. "I want to catch Jessica, just like you do. It doesn't mean I'm ready to forgive you."

I combed through everything in our A-frame. I felt a smidge guilty about touching all of the other girls' things. I shuddered a little when I saw Amanda's journal. I swear, I didn't open it! When April was searching, it must've just flopped open.

There were about a thousand trilobite sketches. Some of them had hearts where the eye sockets should be.

Finally everything was back where it had been and still no stolen goods.

I joined April outside. At least, I tried to. I walked all around the A-frame and couldn't find her anywhere. "April?" I whispered.

"Here!" she hissed back.

One thing about April hasn't changed. When she's into something, she's *way* into it. I spotted her climbing the side of our A-frame. It sounds harder than it actually is, I guess, since the frame is made of wide logs. She swept her hands between the logs. I stepped back when a spider drifted down toward me.

"Are you sure that's a good move for the recently concussed?" I called.

April landed quiet as a cat beside me. "Keep looking."

I grabbed a flashlight from my bag and checked under the A-frame. Nothing.

"Let's think!" April said. "The bracelet! When Jessica found it, she had to have gotten it from somewhere."

"But she never left the A-frame," I said. "Not really."

"She found it on the stoop!"

Both of us rushed to the front of the A-frame. I could see April's hands shaking as she tugged on the planks. Sure enough, one popped up.

We cheered when we saw the pile of stolen items underneath the step. April and I even gave each other a quick hug. Then I ruined it by holding on a bit too long. April stiffened and pushed me away. "Let's just see what's in here."

Carefully, I lifted out Amanda's trilobite. April fished out her laptop and Kira's makeup bag. We put them on my bed. "We did it!" I squealed. "We figured it out!"

"I know!" April said. "We did it!"

It was just like old times.

But when we went back to the stoop to get the rest of the stuff, Jessica stood in front of us, arms crossed. "What do you think you're doing?"

April's face paled and she stepped back toward the bunks. For as fierce she can be when she's sparring, she really backs off when someone's angry.

"Look!" I made my voice as angry as Jessica's. "We know you're the one who stole all of our stuff. Now that you've been fired—"

"Thanks to you!" Jessica stormed.

"You think you can get away with this, but you can't. We caught you. Now we're going to Mr. Bosserman, and you're going to tell him the truth!"

Slowly I felt April move toward me. Her hand shook when she put it on my back, but it seemed to help her gather some courage. "Yeah, Jessica. It's over. You're leaving anyway. Just turn yourself in."

Jessica's eyes darted between us. "I hate kids. Especially spoiled rotten ones. What kind of kid needs designer bags, sneakers, and laptops?" She blew out all the air in her lungs. "Fine," she said. "Fine! Let's go."

"Where?" I asked.

She huffed and puffed again. "To Mr. Bosserman, like you said. I'll own up to it."

Everyone was heading back from the mess hall as we left the A-frame. April and I stood on either side of Jessica. If she tried to run for it, we'd be on her like Shemanda to a fossil.

"Hey, over here!" Jessica shouted as the campers and Mr. Bosserman approached. The sun was going down, sending reddish rays across the campsite and into their eyes. A bunch of them squinted in our direction. Jessica waved her arms. "Over here!" she shouted again.

Kind of a strange way to kick off a confession, I thought. April must've felt the same because she flashed me a worried look.

"I've got 'em!" Jessica yelled. "Caught them red handed, bragging about all they stole!"

"What?" I said.

"We caught *you*," April hissed.

Jessica plastered on her kitten-poster-camp-counselor face, all smiles and wide eyes. "Now, now, little camper wampers! Who's going to believe you?"

Mr. Bosserman led us back to the A-frame, where all the stolen goods were still spread out on my bunk. "Tell me what's going on now, onest." He pinned me in place with his angry look. I looked to April for help, but she was pale and shaking. Tears ran down her cheeks.

"April and I—"

"They admitted it," chirped Jessica, clapping her hands. "I came back here when I noticed they were missing. Sure enough, they were talking about how they fooled everyone!"

"Liar! You're a pants-on-fire liar!" I yelled. "*She's* the thief!"

Jessica shook her head and made a sad face. "What would I want with a bunch of kids' stuff?" She turned toward Mr. Bosserman and said, loud enough for all the gathered campers to hear, "This girl has been making trouble since the day she came to camp. It was all a distraction, so we wouldn't focus on how she and her friend here were lifting things from the rest of us!"

"That's not true! Tell her, April!" I pleaded.

April sobbed. "It's not true!" she sputtered, but her shaky voice wasn't convincing, even for me.

"But they don't even like each other," said Kira, who grabbed her bag from my bed and blew some of the dirt off of it. I shot her a thankful smile, but she narrowed her eyes at me.

"Part of the plan," Jessica lied. "I heard them giggling about it. Didn't they come here babbling about being in some sort of pact?"

"Pack!" I stomped my foot. "We're in a pack, not a pact!"

"So you admit it?" Mr. Bosserman lowered himself on the bunk next to mine, suddenly seeming very old and sad.

"No!" I cried. "You don't understand! April and I both were looking for the thief! We found this stuff under the stoop. Jessica is the one who stole everything!"

"Nice try, kid," Jessica said, smiling at me. She turned back toward Mr. Bosserman. "I told her I suspected her last week. I tried to convince her to give back all the stuff she stole. It's why she ran off when we were at the fossil site and threw that stunt at breakfast. It was all a plot to get me fired for suspecting her!"

"Why are you doing this?" I pleaded with her. Suddenly my head throbbed. "Tell them, April!"

It took April a long time to stop crying so hard she couldn't speak. "We didn't do it!" April finally said. "I swear! It was Jessica."

"Take me through the thefts," Mr. Bosserman asked.

"The first was my bag," Kira said. "It was stolen during our first night of camp, while we slept."

Mr. Bosserman's eyes darted to me. I shook my head when I realized what he was thinking: that was the night I'd gone to his caboose. He knew I'd been awake. He knew everyone else was asleep because he had walked me back. I could see the disappointment in his heavy sigh.

"What about the next one?" he asked.

"It was my bracelet," Megan squeaked. "But Jessica found it."

"It must've fallen out of their hiding place," Jessica added.

"No, you got it out of *your* hiding place." I stomped my foot again, but couldn't stop the tears streaking my cheeks.

"Then it was my trilobite necklace!" Amanda held it up, not noticing Mr. Bosserman's shudder as she slipped it back over her neck.

"Amanda, Sheldon!" I turned toward my friends. "You know that we'd never, ever—"

They looked from me to April, then turned to each other. Without a word to us, they disappeared behind the other campers.

Jessica stepped in front of me, blocking my view of anyone but her. "All easy picks. Interesting, isn't it? All these things went missing when one or both of these girls was around?"

"Almost as interesting as *you* being around!" I turned away from her toward Mr. Bosserman. "Think about it! She was here in our cabin, same as me and April! She was the one who took me to the nurse and ducked out during screen time! She's the one who did it! Tell them, Jessica!"

Jessica just smiled.

Mr. Bosserman sighed. "I've got to think on this."

"What's there to think about?" For a second, Jessica's fake smiley mask faltered. Mr. Bosserman saw it, too. I could tell by how he tilted his chin toward her and then let his eyes slide over to us.

"Girls," he said to me and April, "follow me. Jessica, continue packing."

"Wait a sec! You're still going to fire me?"

Mr. Bosserman glared at her. "Regardless of who did what, you were responsible for these girls, and you didn't do your job." He started to leave, stopped, and pointed to a different counselor. "You, keep an eye on her as she packs."

"Phew!" I sighed. "You believe us."

"Never said that," Mr. Bosserman grumped. "Just covering my bases."

Chapter Sixteen

Mr. Bosserman led us to an office at the eMagine mess hall. "Don't think of sneaking off," he said. "I just need some time to sort this through."

I opened my mouth to argue our case again but he held up a stop sign hand. "Save it. I'll have plenty of questions later."

April sunk into one of the office chairs, tears still leaking down her cheeks. "No one believes us!" she cried.

"Well, you didn't exactly help!" I glared at her. "If anything, you made it worse by the way you acted."

"Oh, shut up, Lucy!" she snapped. "I got scared, okay? I don't like arguing!"

"You don't have a problem arguing with me lately!"

April's mouth popped open then snapped shut. "Hmm. You're right." She shifted in her seat. "You're always pointing out that I stink at sticking up for myself and my friends. But I don't have a problem standing up to you."

I spun around in another office seat, wondering what she was getting at. "So?"

"So you were a real jerk, you know that, right?" April crossed her arms. "What you said to me in front of Kira? It was a real mean thing to do. And what you did to Jer and Megan? That's terrible."

I nodded. "Yeah. And I'm sorry. But—"

"You don't get to do that!" she yelled. "You don't get to add 'but' to an apology!"

I wanted to argue, but I couldn't. She was right. I was wrong. "Fine. No buts. I'm sorry."

"Fine," April answered, spinning around in her chair.

In a moment we were both spinning; I spun so fast I got dizzy. I sort of heard Nurse Gabby's voice in my head saying this wasn't a good thing for April's concussion recovery, but I couldn't stop. Soon we were both laughing.

"We shouldn't be having fun!" April gushed. "We're in a little room, accused of stealing."

"Yeah." I giggled back. "And you're mad at me!"

For some reason, this made us both laugh harder, spin faster. In the middle of all the spinning, our chairs bumped, sending us both wheeling toward the wall and slowing to a stop. I let my eyes unfocus as the room kept on swirling even though the chair was still.

"Can I ask you something?" I asked.

April sprawled out in her seat. "Sure."

"Are you SSCPB?"

April nodded.

"All that stuff about figuring out who you want to be? That's what you've been doing these last couple of weeks?"

"Yeah." She sighed. "At Autumn Grove, it's already decided, right? I'm a dork, just like Sheldon, Amanda, you, and Sam. And there's nothing wrong with that." She shot me a look, cutting off my response. "But what if I want to be different? You know, evolve like these fossil species? Even with the pack, I'm tired of getting pushed into lockers. Tired of having to shout everything because no one will listen to all I have to say."

I didn't respond right away, to let her words sink in. "I didn't know you felt that way."

"Well, I do." She turned toward me. "Do you remember a few weeks ago when I got my hair cut? I was so excited, thought I looked really great. No one noticed."

"I noticed."

"Yeah, you did." April half-twirled and then went back. "I don't know what I'm trying to say, exactly. You know, if I went back to school and kicked butt in gym class the way I did here at Field Day, no one would notice. They'd just cheer for Henry, like always, because he's the one we all think of as the good athlete."

I shrugged. "Maybe."

"And if I went to school talking differently or doing my hair differently, it wouldn't matter. I'd still be a dork."

"So?" I said.

"Well, maybe I don't want that. Maybe I don't want to be that April anymore. It's not just that I don't want to be a dork. I like our pack. I just want to be April first. Does that make sense?"

I squished my lips together, trying to sort how I was feeling. Something she wrote as SSCPB came back to me: *Some people don't want you to change. They might like you just the way you were. Or maybe they like how the old you makes them feel.* That was me, all right. I wanted the fun, silly April who said everything in bursts. I liked that April! Little voice piped in that I liked how that April made me feel. I owned up to that and realized it was true. I liked that I had always felt cooler—and, honesty alert, *better*—than that April.

What I read about Sascha not being willing to change popped into my head, too. Was I being like that? Was I the one breaking up the pack, just because I wasn't letting it change?

"I'm sorry, April," I whispered.

"There are a lot of things I still want to work on. You're right that I stink at standing up for myself and my friends," she murmured.

I shrugged. "No one's perfect. Does this mean . . ."

April smiled. "I want us to all be friends. I want to be in the pack. But I'm not going back to Autumn Grove. Mom and Dad signed me up for a charter school in the fall."

"But—" I bit back my anger. This meant I wouldn't see her in the halls anymore! That she'd be going to a whole new school. "Oh," I said instead. "But we'll still see you after school, right?"

April nodded. "Absolutely!"

She grinned and threw back her head. Just like old times, we howled.

A knock at the door choked off our howls.

"What if it's the cops?" I asked.

April started to shake. "I don't think they'd knock."

The door handle turned, and both April and I gasped.

Sam! He stood in the doorway. Real, in the flesh Sam, with wide chocolate eyes, brown curls all messy, smile slow and steady on his real, standing-there-in-the-door-way face. Sam!

"What are you doing here?" I shot to my feet. I rushed forward to hug him, but it was like I ran into an invisible wall of awkwardness. I punched his shoulder instead. He punched me back. "Shouldn't you be in California, doing a triple axel or something?"

"That's ice skating." He smiled, one of his usual happy-to-see-my-friend smiles, and the awkwardness wall broke apart.

"Surprise," Grandma said, with an edge to her voice. She stood just behind Sam. "Sam's gymnastics camp ended yesterday. He convinced his mom to let him spend the rest of the week here, since they'd already registered and paid and all. Supposed to be today's biggest surprise, until Harold tells me my granddaughter is a suspected thief!"

Sam arched an eyebrow at me. "What's going on, Luc?"

April laughed. "Take a seat, Sam, and we'll fill you in. It's going to take a while."

Sam's smile stretched at April's words. "April! Something's different about you!"

"Let's hope it's not kleptomania," Grandma quipped.

❖ ❖ ❖

April and I told Sam what happened, and I mean everything, even the fights. I also spilled about lying to Jer that April liked him and how it ended with April getting a grapefruit concussion. Sam sighed out his nose, but didn't walk away like I worried he might.

Grandma sat in a corner, pretending to ignore us, except for when we got to the part of Jessica turning on us. Then she called Jessica a word I've only heard on cable. "Yeah, such a jerk!" April said, but she didn't use the word jerk. She used the other word. Grandma can be a bad influence.

We kept on talking, right up until our friends-again howl. Sam kicked in his dying-cat howl and we started up again. Grandma muttered, "Crazy kids."

Again, a knock at the door interrupted our pack howl session.

Chapter Seventeen

This time, Ash stood in the doorway. "Mr. Bosserman wants to see you in the computer lab."

My heart hammered. Why would he want to meet there? We followed Ash. Grandma and Sam trailed behind us. When we got to the lab, I was surprised to see Mr. Bosserman and another man standing next to a computer station. Sheldon and Amanda sat at the computer with identical enormous smiles. I think that might've been the first time I breathed since leaving the little office.

"Oh my goodness," Sam whispered. "That's Alan Bridgeway!"

Sure enough, the man beside Mr. Bosserman was his son. He had the same brown eyes, same wide stance, but luckily seemed to have dodged the hairy ears gene. "Irene," Mr. Bosserman nodded to Grandma.

"This is the Irene I've heard so much about?" Mr. Bridgeway stretched out his hand to Grandma to shake.

"Good to meet you, Alan," Grandma said. "Unless you're about to accuse my granddaughter of stealing. She's a lot of things. A thief isn't one of them."

Mr. Bridgeway smiled. "I can see why my dad likes you. He cuts to the chase, too."

I could almost see a new wall of awkwardness being built between Mr. Bosserman and Grandma as his cheeks pinked and she shuffled her arms.

"What are we doing here?" Jessica stepped forward. "These girls should be sent home. The evidence is obvious."

"Quit your rutching, onest," Mr. Bosserman snapped. He gestured to Shemanda. "These two say they have something to show us."

Sheldon bounced a little in his seat and flexed his fingers. "Right!" he said, almost as excited as when he found the trilobite. "It didn't make sense to us that Lucy or April would steal things like sneakers and designer bags . . ."

"And they'd never take my necklace," Amanda added. She held it up, oblivious to all of our shuddering.

"It was all high-end or expensive stuff. Things people could resell," Sheldon continued. "So we went online to auction sites, looking for the things that were taken."

"Sure enough, we found every single thing that was stolen listed!" Amanda finished.

"That doesn't prove anything," Jessica stammered. "I'm sure there are tons of designer bags and sneakers on those sites."

"But only one of these." Again Amanda hoisted up the trilobite. At the same time, Sheldon clicked on a link, bringing up a picture of the necklace on the site, complete with the string threaded through the eye socket.

"Hmm," Mr. Bridgeway said. "That proves that the thief wanted to sell the items, but it doesn't prove who poste the items."

"Right!" Sheldon bounced again. "Turns out the seller has sold a ton of things online." Sheldon clicked on the seller information.

Up popped a picture of Jessica.

Amanda shot to her feet, fists clenched. "*KUMBAYA!*"

"That trilobite is worthless!" Jessica stormed. "Couldn't even get a single bid on it!"

"Not to me, it isn't," Amanda said.

"Why'd you do it?" Mr. Bosserman asked.

Jessica crossed her arms. "Entitled rich kids don't appreciate what they've got."

"Luckily for you, I'm poor," Sheldon snarled.

"Can't believe I got busted by fifth-grade dorks." Then Jessica mashed her lips together like she was fighting to keep her secret in.

Mr. Bosserman shook his head. "Shame on you."

"I hate kids! Hate them!" Jessica screamed, as my pack howled.

Chapter Eighteen

Even though April felt fine, she wasn't allowed to go swimming the next day, Nurse Gabby's orders. ("Swimming is dangerous for the recently concussed," she'd said without looking up from her romance novel.) It was a perfect swimming day, too. Clear blue sky with just a few stretched-out-cotton-ball clouds. Nice and warm without being sizzling. A dozen ducks floated in the water, just out of reach of the swimmers. But out of solidarity, I also stayed dry. Plus, sitting on the shore made for great spying.

I know! I know! I promised to stop meddling. And I will. I mean, I have. But I could watch what was going on with other campers from our shore-side spot without actually interfering. It was all pretty interesting.

Mr. Bosserman and Grandma stood knee deep in the water, both of them scanning the crowd but also cracking each other up. I couldn't hear what they were saying, and probably wouldn't have understood if I'd been close enough to hear the words, but I could see they were happy.

Grandma had moved into our A-frame when Jessica left. She didn't seem at all upset to be giving up the hair net, but Kira complained nonstop about Grandma's chainsaw snoring. I'd asked Grandma if she and Mr. Bosserman were going to stay in touch after camp. "We'll see," she murmured. "And there's always next summer."

"I'm not coming back here," I vowed.

"We'll see," she had repeated.

Ash swam in broad strokes in the middle of the lake, heading toward a little island where Kira sat in the sun. I kept my eye on Megan, who was doggy paddling just behind Ash. Any time he turned around in the water, she'd ducked under like a very shy shark.

April watched them, too. "All this boyfriend/girlfriend stuff? Is it . . . necessary?" She flopped onto her stomach. "Ash asked me to go to the dance with him. I know it's going to upset Megan."

Every year, Camp Paleo held a dance, Mr. Bosserman had announced that morning. He said it's a "waste of time since ain't no one actually dancing. Just standing around awhile, smiling like fools." Half the campers groaned. The other half cheered. I was in the groaning section.

April sighed. "Jer asked me, too, even though he knows you lied about me liking him. Why would anyone even ask someone to go with them? I mean, we all have to be there. It's not like I could say no, or that by saying yes it really means anything."

"Being popular is not all it's cracked up to be." I thought about when I felt pressured into kissing jerkface Tom last year.

"Ugh! I've heard like six people ask someone to go with them already this morning. Speaking of which . . ." She suddenly hopped to standing as Sam walked up the shore.

"Where are you going?" Sam headed toward me. Crap sandwich! What if he asked me to go to the dance? I sort of wanted him to ask me and at the same time didn't. I was so confused you would've thought I was the one with the concussion.

"Bye," April sing-songed and walked off toward a different group of girls.

"Hey." Sam lay beside me, propping himself up on his elbow.

"Hey, yourself."

"So I've been meaning to ask you . . ."

Lollipop farts!

". . . have you seen these ducks? They're terrifying."

"Are you kidding? They're adorbs!" I stood up and flapped my arms. "Here, ducky, ducky! Here ducky, ducky!"

A huge, shining green mallard waddled toward me. "Squawk!"

"Just kidding, duck. I don't have anything."

Sam whimpered behind me. "I hate ducks."

The duck waddled closer. "Squawk!"

"Shoo!" I waved the duck away. Its beak was pretty long. I wondered if ducks have talons. The duck waddled abnormally fast toward us, its wings flapping and beak open.

"Squawk! Squawk! Squawk!"

"It's attacking!" Sam yelped. He grabbed my wrist. "Run! I told you ducks were creepy!"

Sam never asked me to the dance, but we did spend the rest of the day running from mad ducks, skipping rocks, and being friends. And I was totally okay with that.

Even Grandma was in on this dance hysteria.

On the night of the dance, as usual, Grandma wore sandals, but she painted her toenails electric blue. Her ankle-skimming, blue tie-dye dress rounded at her hips. Hmm. Grandma had lost weight recently. She usually sort of looked like a refrigerator box, but now I could definitely see that she had a waist. Come to think of it, I had seen a bunch of yoga DVDs at her house last time I slept over. Grandma's lips shimmered with lip gloss. When did

Grandma wear lip gloss? I wondered if she borrowed it from Kira, who was granting lip gloss to everyone now that her makeup bag was back. Grandma's curly hair, usually a wild mop around her head, was smoothed into soft waves around her face, like you'd see movie stars wearing their hair in vintage movie posters.

"Wow, Grandma," I said. "You look . . ."

"Real pretty." Mr. Bosserman stood at the entrance of the A-frame. He wore a button-down checked shirt and gray pants. "Alan picked this outfit. I wanted to wear my usual camp attire but he—"

Grandma interrupted him. "You look wonderful, Harold."

Mr. Bosserman's chest puffed up. "Shall we?" He held out a hand and Grandma slipped hers into it. But before she left, she leaned toward me. "Maybe put on a dress. Do something with your hair?"

I shrugged.

"Suit yourself," Grandma said as she left.

But I did let April play around with my hair when she asked. She said she wanted to try it out on my head before attempting it for herself. April made a ton of little braids, twisting them around into a pile on top of my head. I reached for the mirror, sure it looked like the time I touched one of those crazy blue electricity balls at the science museum.

Kira batted the mirror away. "Stop!" She dumped her makeup bag onto the cot. "Let me do a few things first." Now I knew they were playing a joke on me. Kira hated me. She ran brushes along my cheeks, smeared something onto my lips, and curled my lashes. "This doesn't mean we're friends," she said as she handed me the mirror. "But now we're even for you finding my bag before Jessica made off with it."

The girl in the mirror—she was me, but not me.

This girl's hair was wicked cool. Blonde streaks wove through the braids. Guess I spent more time in the sun than I thought. The mirror girl's eyes were wide and lashes long. Her skin shimmered. She was . . .

"Real pretty." Amanda stood just behind me.

"Thanks." I smiled. "You look great, too."

And she did. I didn't even know Amanda owned a dress, but she stood there in a blue sundress, her hair pulled back in a bun, her trilobite hanging from her neck. Sheldon was going to swoon.

"Aren't you going to do your braids?" I asked April.

"I changed my mind."

Kira immediately began tugging at her braids. I didn't roll my eyes, but just barely.

We left the A-frame and ran almost right into Sam. "Hey!" he said. "You look great."

"You look surprised."

"It's just, you don't normally have a shiny mouth."

"Oh."

"Oh."

More bricks stacked up on our wall of awkwardness.

Mr. Bosserman was right that most people didn't dance at the annual dance. Maybe it had something to do with the music, which blasted from the Fanilow eMagine camper's iPad.

But Sheldon and Amanda boogied away in the middle of the room, arms flailing and legs kicking. Jer bounced a little beside them. When a slow song played, Sheldon and Amanda kept on with their upright seizure dancing. A few couples went out to the dance floor, sort of drifting side to side together, arms stretched out as far as they could go in order to reach the others' shoulders.

Sam and I sat to the side, watching everyone but talking about Sascha and Ralph. Sam said he'd email Mr. Able for an update when we got home. "So do you want to?" he asked as another slow song came on.

"Uh—"

"Go visit the wolves this summer, I mean? Mom said she'd take us again." Sam took a drink of punch. "I think she liked it as much as we did last time."

"Yeah." I nodded. "I'd love that, actually."

Across the dance floor, Megan trailed behind Ash, who filled up two cups with punch. *Please let one be for Megan.* I crossed my fingers for my shy friend. But when Ash whipped around, Megan stood so close to him that he quickly backed up and some of the red juice splattered onto his white shirt. She reached out for one of the cups anyway. "Thanks!" I heard her say. "Want to dance?"

"Wait! What?" He flicked some of the punch off his hands.

Megan's lips shook. "Want to dance?" she squeaked.

Ash looked at her like she had a trilobite for a face. "No." He took the cup back out of Megan's hand and called April's name.

In a second, Sam was on his feet. "What are you doing?" I hissed, but he ignored me. Instead, he walked straight to Megan.

"Would you please dance with me?" he asked, and grabbed her hand.

The two of them went to the dance floor, Megan's smile outshining the tears in her eyes.

Chapter Nineteen

Megan whispered my name in the dark.

"What?" I whispered back.

"Can I ask you something?"

She didn't have to. I knew what she was going to say. I could tell the minute Sam had taken her hand. Just as quick as she had fallen for Jer, then Ash, now she was head over heels for Sam. "Do you think I should ask Sam for his email? So we can stay in touch?"

"Sure," I said. "Go for it." But I sort of wanted to punch her in the face. I'm not sure why. I rolled onto my other side.

"You seem mad," Megan whispered a minute later.

"I'm not mad," I hissed back.

"Well, you seem mad."

"Of course she's mad," Kira snapped from above Megan. "Duh. She and Sam are a thing, even if neither wants to admit it. Back off, Megan. Latch onto someone else."

"That's not true!" I sat up in bed, whapping my head on April's bunk.

Amanda groaned next to us. "Yes, it is!"

April's head popped down over her bunk. "If you're not ready to admit it, that's fine. But if you're not okay with Megan getting closer to him, you should admit that."

"Fine," Megan said. "I think I like Jer more anyway. We sort of hit it off thanks to April's grapefruit concussion."

"Fine," I said.

"Go. To. Sleep," Grandma said. I knew why she was so sleepy. Halfway through the dance, I'd noticed that she and Mr. Bosserman were missing. Sam and I sneaked down the path to the caboose. Sure enough, the old farts were dancing under the twinkling lights.

On our last night at Camp Paleo, we had another campfire dinner. The sky was clear and black, peppered with stars. I crossed my fingers that we'd get to have mountain pies, this time cooked. But instead, Mr. Bosserman asked us all to bring out the can of soup we had been asked to pack. I looked for my can of bean with bacon soup and wondered how Mr. Bosserman was going to manage to find twenty pots so each of us could cook our dinners. Oops. Twenty-one pots, counting Sam.

"You're awfully happy about stone soup," Grandma said as I unearthed my can from the bottom of my duffel bag.

"Stone soup?" I asked. Grandma just laughed.

At the campfire, Kira held up her minestrone soup. "It's just like April's!" she gushed. "We have excellent taste."

Jer kind of hid his split pea and ham soup behind his back, only showing it when Mr. Bosserman made everyone go around the circle and say what they brought. "It's pretty green," he said.

Megan, sitting beside him, held out her own can of split pea. They smiled at each other. "Green's my favorite color," she squeaked.

"I set them up," I whispered to Sam.

"I thought you set him up with April?" He scanned the circle. "And didn't you say you tried to put Megan with Ash?"

"Yes, but the grapefruit concussion I caused brought them together."

"And you totally planned that, right?"

He smiled, and I grinned back. But when we didn't break eye contact that wall began to rebuild, awkward brick by awkward brick. It only broke apart when April handed me a can opener. "Mr. Bosserman said we need to open all of our cans."

"Every one of you brought something to this camp. Special skills, talents, whatnot. All of them came together like a big vat of soup, making a brand new flavor." I did not like where I thought this was headed. My grip on my beans and bacon tightened. "So on this last day of camp, we're each going to add our own flavor soup to dinner." He hoisted a gigantic cauldron over the flames. "We're making stone soup, bringing together everything we've got."

Minestrone, tomato, split pea, bean and bacon, ham and cheese, chicken noodle, beef barley, and Italian wedding soups make a terrible analogy. I liked Mr. Bosser-man's little speech; we did all come together in the end. But even Dad would be disgusted by this concoction. "I know where Grandma keeps some cookies," I whispered to Sam as our soup got cold.

We backed away from the campfire, quiet as ninjas, and snuck back to the A-frame. I know, I know, I'd promised no more sneaking off. But if I was sneaking with someone else, then it wasn't really sneaking off by myself. Right? Whatever. Sam waited outside while I grabbed Grandma's secret stash.

Holding a chocolate chip cookie up to toast, I clinked it against Sam's oatmeal raisin. "To us!" I said.

The word "us" seemed to echo in the night air. More bricks stacked on our wall.

"Do you feel that?" Sam asked.

I shoved the cookie in my mouth.

"I feel like every time we get anywhere close to talking about *feelings*," his face scrunched up like the word tasted like curdled milk, "things get weird between us."

I shoved another cookie in my mouth.

"Listen." He grabbed my wrists and lowered them from my face. Globs of cookie fell out of my mouth. *Please don't kiss me! Please don't kiss me!* I don't think I'd recover from another bad kiss. Sam laughed instead. "You're a total mess."

"I know," I garbled around the cookie.

He sighed. "Please just listen and don't get all weird on me." He cocked an eyebrow like he just remembered who he was talking to. "Weirder than usual," he amended, dropping my wrists. "I don't want a girlfriend. I want a friend."

I let out a breath I didn't know I was holding. Again, a stone soup of happy and sad gurgled in my belly.

"But *if* I wanted a girlfriend, which I don't, I'd want her to be you."

The stone soup was happy. Just happy. Sam bumped my shoulder. I bumped him back.

The wall of awkwardness shattered, each brick blasted away.

Did we howl? Of course we did.

Acknowledgments

Thank you, Mom and Dad, for sending me to summer camp when I was ten. I know I never actually said these words to you—or any words at all, in fact, for several hours after you picked me up. Back then, I was consumed with figuring out what I had done to cause you to send me to "live like a pioneer" for two weeks. Maybe I still was in mourning for what would've been the world's greatest mountain pie but, thanks to a sudden downpour dampening the campfire and my culinary dreams, it became just soggy bread with cheese and tomato sauce. Or perhaps, now that I was in the tight quarters of our car alongside my equally sullen, stinky sister, beginning the leg of our five-hour drive home,

I was too busy regretting not opening that pack of soap you had slipped into my suitcase.

How could I have known then that someday that mosquito-filled forest of awkwardness would provide the inspiration to create *Camp Dork*?

So, now that your fateful words ("Someday you will thank me for this experience, Beth") have come to fruition, here you go: You were right.

Be sure to check out other books by Beth Vrabel
from Sky Pony Press!

"You won't want to stop reading about Lucy and her pack…a heartwarming story to which everyone can relate." —**ELIZABETH ATKINSON**, author of *I, Emma Freke*

pack

of

dorks

B E T H   V R A B E L

After a failed kiss behind the ball shed, Lucy is propelled from coolest to lamest fourth grader overnight. Now, Lucy is trapped in Dorkdom. Will she ever escape? Or will Lucy be surprised to find what being a dork really is all about?

Paperback * $7.99 * ISBN: 978-1-5107-0179-3 *
Available wherever books are sold

A BLIND GUIDE TO STINKVILLE

BETH VRABEL

author of *Pack of Dorks*

When Alice moves across the company to a new town, her albinism, and the blindness that goes with it, is truly a disability for the first time. But she's set on proving to her family, her friends, and her town that there is more to her than just a blind girl with a farting dog and walking stick.

Hardcover * $16.99 * ISBN: 978-1-63450-157-6 *
Available wherever books are sold